Again

R. N. CAUSSEAUX

authorHOUSE®

AuthorHouse™
1663 Liberty Drive
Bloomington, IN 47403
www.authorhouse.com
Phone: 1-800-839-8640

First published by AuthorHouse   4/21/2011

ISBN: 978-1-4567-6025-0 (e)
ISBN: 978-1-4567-6026-7 (sc)

Printed in the United States of America

This story is dedicated to my soul mate. My most heart felt wish is that we could have been together longer but one lifetime doesn't last long enough to fulfill that wish. So I wait until next time with love.

Earth Year 1755

Aspen came out of the wooded area and viewed the tranquil scene before him. Rachel sat in the green meadow surrounded by wild flowers. The brilliant hues of red, yellow and purple were scattered through the lush grass in some places and clumped in solid groups in others. Iridescent rainbow butterflies danced on the warm breeze. Rachel softly brushed one from the page she was reading. Aspen didn't want to disturb this tranquility, but he had to. He walked to her side and lowered himself to the ground.

"Enjoying your reading?"

"Very much." Smiling, she laid the bound papers on the grass, stretched her arms and clasped her hands around her knees. "Shakespeare improves with every play he writes. He hadn't finished this one the last time I was here." Rachel lay back on the grass and watched the butterflies float against the deep blue background of the sky. Aspen inhaled deeply and savored the not quite sweet aroma of the flowers and grass.

"I bring a message," Aspen said quietly. His reluctance was obvious as he paused longer than was necessary. "They say it's time to go back."

"So soon?" Rachel turned over on her stomach and plucked idly at the grass. "It seems like I just got here."

Aspen chuckled. "When you picked the mother, you should have chosen someone younger. She's ready now." Aspen could feel her longing to stay that came from deep within.

Rachel sat up. Her gaze slowly swept across the meadow as though memorizing each sight, each color. When she spoke, it was with the wistful tone of a child.

"Do you think I'll ever learn enough so I don't have to go back? You know how it is there. I was so lonely last time and didn't even have you to talk to. Oh, now I know you were there, but I didn't know it then, and I won't know it this time unless I get a lot smarter or at least start to understand better."

Aspen laid his hand on her shoulder. "There will come a time when you have learned enough, but I don't know when that will be. Only They can judge that. Until then, I will be with you, and maybe this time you will realize that."

"When do I go before Them for my reversion?"

"They're waiting now." Aspen stood and offered his hand to Rachel.

With a resigned sigh she took his hand and stood, then bent to retrieve the papers from the ground.

"I guess I'll have to finish reading this when I get back." They walked up the knoll away from the meadow and were among the trees when Rachel spoke again.

"I think I'll ask Them to give me a soul mate this time so I won't be so lonely."

The words brought Aspen to a halt. He took Rachel's arm and turned her toward him.

"A soul mate is a very big responsibility and can cause heartache if it doesn't work out while you're there."

The intensity of Aspen's response surprised Rachel.

"I'll just have to make it work out," she said. "Anyway, it's better than being lonely all the time. I'm willing to take the chance."

Her statement sounded confident though a flicker of doubt showed in her eyes.

"Rachel, once you have a soul mate, the love between you will last forever. Have you even begun to understand what forever means? You'll put his wants, needs and happiness before your own. It will greatly alter your free will. Anytime you have a major decision to make in your life on Earth, you'll think first about how it will affect your soul mate. This may alter your decisions, therefore altering the course of your life."

Aspen maintained his hold on her arm and searched her mind to see if she understood his words. The understanding was there but it was infused with the dread of returning and the remembrance of the aching loneliness.

Rachel covered his hand on her arm with her own and slowly removed it, but continued to hold it.

2

"I know you only want the best for me, Aspen. You want me to be as happy as possible while I'm learning. I'll try to do the right thing. We better go now and not keep Them waiting."

They walked on and soon reached the great hall where Rachel was to meet with Them. Before going in she turned and put her arms around her beloved guardian.

"If the time to leave is as close as you say, I may not see you before I go. Be with me, Aspen, and pray I make the best choices for this lifetime." Rachel entered the building alone.

Chapter 1

1755

He fetched the midwife in the afternoon when his wife said it was time. The night stretched long, but the old, stooped midwife assured them everything was going fine and the child would soon appear.

The weather was too warm for the fire burning in the fireplace, but the fire was needed to boil the pot of water hanging over it. The firelight also helped the two bedside candles push back the darkness in the cabin. He had made a pot of strong tea from their scant tea supply, and drank it nervously through the night. Now the pot sat almost empty on the hearth.

He stood by the bed where his young wife sweated in the twisted covers. Her belly was huge with the child struggling to be born. The midwife sat beside her. Fatigue showed on the faces of all three.

Aspen hovered patiently in the corner, waiting as he had waited several times before. His glow was unnoticed. If the people in the room had noticed, they would dismiss it as being from the fire or the candles. People always gave explanations to their minds for things they didn't comprehend.

Another glow sank through the ceiling and hesitated before joining Aspen in the corner. This too went unnoticed by the three people.

"Who are you?" Aspen asked. "I wasn't told this would require two guardians."

"I'm Willow. I've brought part of another, born just tonight, to put into this one to make them soul mates. I'll need to take part of her to put into him."

"When was this decided and why wasn't I told before now?"

Willow's golden glow tinged slightly pink. "That's my fault. They told me to find you and tell you several days ago, but I'm new at this. Got my guardian angel certification just two weeks ago. Did you know there is a guardian named Espen on the other side of the Earth? Well, now I've found you, and there's plenty of time to make the exchange. My boy, Edward, is only a few miles over the mountain."

Aspen smiled at Willow. He remembered how nervous he had been as a new guardian, waiting for Rachel to be born the first time. He also remembered the comment she made about a soul mate. Such decisions were never made by Them until the soul was back on Earth, and firmly implanted in the chosen mother. He thought it odd They had decided this union was to be with a new soul, and not an older one who had also requested a soul mate. Edward must be someone special.

"Where are their guardians?" Willow gestured to the humans.

"They just stepped out for a minute. Childbirth is hard on a mother's guardian. I know." Aspen was quiet for a while as he remembered the times Rachel had given birth in other lives. He gave himself a small shake and brought his mind back to the present.

"Did you have any problem taking the part from Edward that will go into Rachel? It's been several lifetimes since I had my training."

"No problem. The father's guardian coached me a little, but it's really easy."

Three more golden glows now materialized in the room, close to the bed. Seconds later a small mewing cry announced Rachel's arrival.

Aspen and Willow worked quickly. Aspen brushed his hand through the infant and brought out the small part needed. Willow followed, and replaced the missing part with the one brought from Edward. Rachel stopped crying. With only a slight hesitation, Aspen relinquished the part of Rachel he held. Willow took it and held it gently against his breast.

Willow floated toward the ceiling. "I'll be seeing you soon, I'm sure."

Aspen tried not to be worried as a part of his charge was taken from the room. "Yes, we'll see each other soon and often. God speed."

The midwife did her job without hesitation and handed the bundled baby girl to the father.

He accepted her with a broad grin. "If I didn't know better, I'd swear the babe was smiling. You done good, darlin'. You done give us the most beautiful baby girl ever born in these mountains." The mother and father's eyes locked, both filled with love and happy tears.

The four golden glows in the room could not suppress the increased brightness this moment brought.

"It's getting pretty light. Must be close to sun-up." The father laid Rachel in her mother's arms. "Better get out to the shed and tend to the stock."

Rachel's new life began, with a soul mate somewhere over the mountain.

****

1761

"Edward, this sure would be a good spot for our cabin when we get growed up and married."

Six year old Rachel and Edward sat in a deeply shaded area with their bare feet in the cool water of a small stream.

"Naw, ain't enough flat land for farming. We might not get married, no how." Edward's cheeks showed a slight blush under his tan.

"Pa would let us use some of his land. It ain't all cleared yet. And I know we'll get married cause we was born on the same day. You're just a couple hours older than me." Rachel pushed her dark hair away from her face. "Besides, I done decided you was the one I'm marrying."

Edward stood up and retrieved a fruit jar sitting by a tree. "I best be getting on home. Ma will skin me if I don't get back with this medicine for Grandma's ague. Thank your ma again for letting us have some. She makes the best brew for curing in these parts. Everybody says so."

"No thanks needed. Pa sets aside a patch of his corn every year for Ma's medicine. She's real smart about that."

"Well, bye." Edward started his long walk home.

Willow left his place in the tree where he and Aspen had been watching the children.

"I wouldn't mind a taste of that medicine myself," *he told Aspen laughing.*

Aspen grinned and shook his head. "Sometime I think you should have been made a human soul instead of a guardian angel." *He flipped a wingtip as a sign of farewell and left the tree to follow Rachel.*

A slight disturbance made Aspen turn back. Willow was bent to the ground. He gently held a copperhead snake against the ground only a few inches from Edward's footstep. He grinned back at Aspen as Edward went on his way, completely unaware of the poisonous viper so close.

****

1772

Edward and Rachel stood in the door of their cabin. The last guests were disappearing down the trail. Edward hesitantly put his arm around Rachel's waist and drew her closer to his side.

A teasing smile danced on his lips and in his dark eyes. "We got us a cabin right where you wanted it. We done got married jist like you wanted. Now what else do you want?"

"I'd like to cook us our first meal in our own place but, with all the food left over from the wedding that would be a waste. So I guess I just want my husband to kiss me like a husband's supposed to." Rachel turned in his arm and pressed her body against him.

"Oh, Rachel, I do love you with all my heart and soul."

The sun sank behind the next mountain. The soft shadows of evening enveloped the cabin. The couple no longer stood in the door. It was closed. Soft glows shone from the peak of the roof.

"How long do you think we'll have to stay out here?" *Willow asked from his seat on the roof.*

Aspen chuckled. "Better get comfortable and settle in for the night. We've got some beautiful scenery to enjoy." *He gazed at the silhouetted trees, dark against the orange-pink sky.*

The two guardians watched as the sky became dark and millions of stars scattered across the canvas of heaven. They were happy with the day that had just ended, happy with the night, happy with their human charges.

****

1774

Rachel clung to Edward's arm with tears streaming down her face. "I can't believe you're doing this, leaving me and little Joseph here on this mountain by ourselves. That war don't mean nothing to us. It's miles and miles away. It ain't never going to get close to here. And if it does, who's going to be here to protect your wife and child? Your Pa gave you that old gun to shoot squirrel and deer, to provide for your family. Now you're thinking about shooting men. The Good Book says you ain't supposed to kill. What's gonna happen if you do and I get to heaven and start looking around for you and you'll be burning below? And what if you get yourself killed? What will become of us then?" Joseph joined her plea with his own wails, his face buried in her skirt and his tiny fists balled in the fabric. He didn't understand what was going on but he had never seen his mother like this and reacted accordingly.

Edward tried to pull Rachel to him with his free arm but she kept her stance, looking into his face.

"I ain't going to get myself killed. Rachel, honey, you have to understand. If we don't stop them redcoats, the king of England his self will be over here telling us what we can and can't do. You don't want Joseph growing up and having to bow down to some king that don't have no business being here anyway. Do you? Now I'm jist going to join up with the other men and when them soldiers see us all standing there saying you can't take over our homes, they'll go back to England and that will settle that. There's plenty of firewood cut and plenty of food. I'll be back before it runs out. And if I see it's going to take longer, I'll run on back home and stock you up again. Your Ma and Pa are jist a short walk down the trail so you ain't really by yourself. This has to be done, Rachel, so dry up the tears and send me on my way with a smile and a kiss. I've got to go."

Rachel collapsed against Edward's chest at the finality of his words. She buried her face in his shirt. She loosened the ties that held the shirt closed and breathed in the scent of his body. The memory of that would have to stay with her through all the lonely nights ahead.

"Rachel, it's early autumn. I feel sure I'll be home before the worst of winter sets in." Edward gathered his traveling gear in preparation for the job ahead of him. With Rachel's tears still damp on his shirt, he set off at a fast pace, turning only once to wave at the woman holding his son in her arms in front of their snug cabin.

As his arm lowered from that wave, he muttered, "Maybe I shouldn't be leaving. It don't feel good even if it feels right to go." With a shake of his head he dislodged the thought and another replaced it. "I've never been off this mountain. All I know are the stories the traders and travelers tell. Cities with hundreds of people. Stores side by side on both sides of a road where you can see and buy any do-dad ever made." He touched the pouch hanging around his neck containing the few coppers he had accumulated in his life. "I'll buy Rachel the prettiest thing I see so she'll get over being mad at me for going."

"I don't like this." Aspen hovered slightly above Willow who followed Edward down the path. From this vantage point he could keep an eye on Rachel, still standing by the cabin.

"I don't either," Willow replied. "But I can't get through to him. This freewill thing humans have sure makes it hard on us. He really thinks he's doing the right thing. Maybe he is. I don't understand war and killing."

Aspen floated to the tops of the trees. "Well, God speed you both back soon." He watched until the man and his guardian were out of sight.

1775

Edward saw the cities. There was one just across the bay from where he was now. It was called Boston and he was on a place called Breeds Hill. Those few coppers he would have spent on Rachel were long gone, spent instead on food that was also long gone. His hunger was slacked only a little by the bottle of water hanging from his shoulder by a strap. He took a small sip to dampen the dryness in his mouth that came from the heat and fear that hovered about him. He didn't know what day it was or even what month, but it was hot summer. The wood and meat supply he left Rachel was surely gone by now. The men he traveled with had gone farther and farther from his quiet mountain, and joined with other groups. They sometimes hunted the enemy but more often were chased by the organized military of King George III.

The dreaded British drums began. Daylight pinked the sky.

"My God, what am I doing here?" Edward crouched lower in the ditch he and the other men had dug during the night.

The man to Edward's left turned to him with a sick grin. The first cannon volley was discharged from a ship in the harbor below. Part of the man's head vanished in a bloody eruption.

"I'm in hell. Rachel, I'm sorry." Edward screamed these words as the advancing enemy charged.

The man to his right pitched backward, a red spot on his shoulder. He was a stranger, another American caught up in the fight. Edward quickly moved to his side and tore his shirt away to examine the wound. The bullet had gone completely through. The torn shirt made a quick bandage that helped to stop the flow of blood. He lifted the man's head and gave him a drink of the precious water. The cork was firmly back in the bottle when another enemy bullet found its mark. Blackness engulfed Edward.

"Who are you? What happened?" Edward floated some feet off the ground, his arm firmly held by Willow. He looked below and saw his body slumped over another man, completely covering that man's upper body and head.

"Everything is all right now. We're going to take a short journey and leave this place of killing." Willow moved closer and put his arm around Edward's shoulder.

"Thank God for that. But ... I don't understand. What's happening?"

"That was a very brave thing you did - turning your back on your enemy to help another. The man you helped will survive. He was saved for a purpose unknown to me." Willow's glow encircled them both. "We must leave now. You will understand soon."

Edward thought fleetingly of Rachel but was quickly encompassed by a feeling of love and serenity as they floated away from the scene of carnage below.

****

Rachel bent to her task in the small garden beside the cabin. Joseph still slept soundly inside. She would hear him when he woke and called for her. All the vegetables seemed to get ready for picking at the same time. She had begun the day's work as soon as it was light enough to see the ripe peas on their vines. A sharp pain suddenly ripped through her body as if a part of her was being torn away. She collapsed to her knees and a single wail issued from her lips.

"Edward!" He was dead. She knew it. A part of herself had been killed.

Aspen hovered close, helpless to ease the pain coursing through Rachel.

"Oh, my sweet Rachel. I tried to warn you. Having a soul mate can cause great pain - the pain you are feeling now." He encircled Rachel with his arms and looked skyward. "Please, God. Help Rachel. Give me the power and wisdom to help her."

The news of Edward's death eventually reached the mountain. Edward and Rachel's parents provided for her and Joseph. She refused to leave her little cabin to live with either of them. A few years passed and she married another man. He was a good man, a good husband, a good father to Joseph. She had other children and grew older. She became a grandmother and grew older still. The sweet memory of her brief time with Edward stayed in her heart as a secret treasure. A shady spot above the cabin became her final resting place when she was free at last to go in search of him, her soul mate.

"Hello, Aspen. It's good to see you again."

Aspen folded Rachel into his arms. "Shush now, and rest until I get you home." He began the ascent.

Rachel chuckled. "You know better than to shush me, if I'm on Earth or at home. This time I felt you and knew you were with me in those last years. I didn't know who you were, but it was a big comfort just knowing you were there, and I could talk to you."

"And I answered but you didn't always hear me."

"Where is Edward? They didn't make him go back before I got there, did they?"

"Of course not. You'll have some time together. But you know the

rules. *The pickup must be made by the guardian alone. Some are a little disoriented when they first leave their human bodies. You were a few times.*"

Rachel nestled her head against her beloved guardian's chest. "This time I was waiting for you."

Aspen settled Rachel softly onto the receiving area and turned to face the two hurrying toward them.

Edward and Rachel fell into each other's arms and held tightly in silence. They finally pulled apart enough to grin broadly.

"I love you," Edward said softly.

"I love you," Rachel answered.

Edward turned her slightly. "This is Willow, my guardian. I've already met Aspen."

Rachel extended her hand to Willow. "Hello Willow. I'm glad to finally meet you."

Willow took Rachel's hand in both of his. "The pleasure is mine, and I truly mean that."

"Come on, Rachel," Edward said as he tugged on her other hand. "I want to show you something. It's fantastic."

Rachel laughed at his excitement. "All right, but I may have already seen it. Remember, I've been here before – several times."

They turned and walked away, their arms around each other, leaving Willow and Aspen to follow, or not.

Chapter 2

1830

Six-year-old Rachel sat on the bluff and gazed across the wide expanse of water. She loved it when Mama sent her down by the Ohi to look for fresh spring greens. Some parents wouldn't let their children play by the treacherous, fast moving river, but Rachel had been born there. The river was the way of life for her. Their first cabin had been just across from where Licking River joined the Ohi. Now they lived in a bigger cabin a little further west where more people had built and Mama had the company of other ladies when Pap was gone on his river trips.

Last year Pap let her oldest brother, Tommy, go with him when he did his trading up and down the Ohi. Tommy came home with exciting tales and small treasures for each member of the family. Rachel listened wide-eyed and, in the first lull of talk, asked Pap when she could go with him.

"Reckon you better wait till you're nine or ten, same as Tommy now." Pap laughed as he said it.

"Don't be filling the child's head with ideas like that," Mama scolded. "In case you hadn't noticed, she's a girl. No daughter of mine will be going off on that boat of yours to God knows where meeting God knows who."

Rachel didn't understand why Mama was so fussy about her. She was the only girl and her three brothers always seemed to have more fun. Mama even made her bathe more often and change her dress every few days. She wasn't allowed to wear cut off pants like the boys wore in the summertime. Her big ambition at age six was to grow up to be a man, or at least get to act like one.

Rachel suddenly stopped her daydreaming and turned to face east. A peculiar thrill ran through her body and it seemed to come from that direction. For some unexplained reason she began to laugh and run along the riverbank, swishing the bag of greens over her head.

"Yes, he's on earth again, Rachel." Aspen knew Rachel couldn't hear him with her ears, but he knew she felt the meaning without knowing what it was.

*****

1836

Edward loved his Grandpapa who never yelled at him or his older sister, Annie. He always gave them a pence for candy at Christmas and Easter. But he yelled at Papa. He yelled so much that Papa didn't listen anymore. Grandpapa had made it hard on Papa ever since he married Mama. There were always arguments and fights between the two houses only a few doors from each other. Annie was ten and old enough to act like Mama when the yelling started – frown and leave the room.

Annie was almost grown, and already had a job doing chores for the old lady on the next lane. The old lady's son sent her money from London but the government dole people knew nothing of that. She begged Annie to stay with her when Papa said the family was going to America, but Mama wouldn't hear of it.

Papa said he was tired of Grandpapa yelling that he didn't work hard enough or make enough money. Grandpapa told everyone that Papa didn't buy enough food or coal, and he didn't go to confession every week.

Edward knew they were sometimes a little hungry and a little cold, but wasn't everyone? At least everyone on their lane. And what sins did his strong, wise Papa have to confess?

So Papa said they were leaving Ireland and going to America, and Grandpapa yelled.

"You'll come crawling back, and what will you find here? Sold your

16

house and all that was in it. You'll not like what you find in that heathen country but there's no stopping you. Don't think we'll take you in when you come home without a jar to pee in and no window to throw it out of."

Grandmama assured them in a tearful whisper, when Grandpapa was out of the room, "There will always be a place for you when you return."

Papa assured her, in a loud voice, "We will not be back."

Grandmama cried into her apron all the way to the dock. "I'll never see me daughter or grandchildren again."

Grandpapa would not come to the dock.

Edward watched as long as he could see her standing on the dock as the ship sailed away. He really didn't want to leave her or Grandpapa. He didn't want to leave his friends. America was far, far away across an ocean, on the other side of the world. Edward was frightened.

. . .

The sun was brilliant on the white capping waves but it gave little warmth against the chill. Edward leaned over the bow of the ship letting the spray drench him while he held to the top rail. He was cold but laughter bubbled out of him, and he felt the first real joy of the whole trip.

The captain said they would reach New York by tonight and he strained his eyes for the first glimpse of land.

"Hold tight, little Edward. Can't have you falling over now that you're this close to Rachel." Willow had a firm grip on Edward's coat and smiled at his young charge's happiness. It would be a while yet before the soul mates met again but he was happy to think about that time and seeing his old friend, Aspen.

. . .

1842

Edward listened intently from his bed in the loft. Mama and Papa had

17

been arguing ever since he was sent up early, the way he always was when they had something important to talk about.

Mama's words were halting, interspersed with sobs. "If you don't want to stay here, we can go back to Ireland. You know the last letter from home said Father was very sick. And you know Annie's husband won't go further west with us. He said he might go back to Ireland if we do. They'd live only a few miles from us on his family's farm. You want us to leave everything again, our home, our friends. Edward is almost finished with his schooling. Think about what you're asking."

Papa's voice was wheedling. "But it will be better, a better job, a better home. Didn't I make the right decision to come to the new country and haven't things been better. It's a beautiful town. They call it the Queen City of the west. The pay is much more than I make now. We can start saving a little for our old age. And the house that comes with the job must be really grand. He said it has four rooms and a nice yard. You can have a garden again, like back home." His voice changed and became very stern. "I've told the man yes and he's expecting us in a month, so you best start packing what you want to take in the morning. There'll be no more tears or arguments."

Edward heard the familiar sounds from below of his parents preparing for bed. The stove door creaked as it was opened to bank the fire. The board was dropped in place to secure the front door. The bed squeaked as one of his parents sat on it. His papa's boots clunked as they hit the floor. It became dark when the lamp was put out. All was quiet except for the soft sound of Mama's rocker, back and forth. In his mind Edward could see her sitting in the dark in front of the stove. He didn't want to think about moving again. The rhythmic sound of the rocker lulled his eyes closed and he slept.

. . .

"A new family is moving in. Maybe they'll have a son you won't think is dumb." Rachel's mother rinsed a shirt and handed it to Rachel to wring and hang on the garden fence.

"Why are you and Pap always looking for a man for me? Do you want to get rid of me? You'd have to do the wash by yourself if I wasn't here." Rachel grinned to take the edge off her words.

"We aren't trying to get rid of you but you're eighteen, and probably the oldest single girl in the whole town except for a few really ugly ones.

It's time you had a husband and gave us a few more grandchildren. The boys had no problem finding mates and giving me babies to cuddle and rock like a grandmother is supposed to."

"Someday, Mama, I promise. When the right man comes along I'll marry him straight away and start popping out babies so fast you won't be able to catch them all." Rachel deliberately turned away from Mama as she said this to hide a mischievous grin.

"Rachel! It's talk like that drives the boys away. Will you ever start acting like a lady?"

"Ladies don't have any fun. If it will make you feel better, as soon as the wash is finished I'll bake something for the new neighbors and take it over to them." Rachel took another shirt from the rinse water and wrung it. She hummed a tune and carefully laid it over the fence.

Mama watched her with a frown, then sighed, shook her head and put her hands back in the water. She just couldn't understand this beautiful daughter who seemed in an exceptionally good mood this morning.

Rachel had run off every young suitor that called on her since the age of fifteen. Some left crest fallen while others left angry, with Rachel's laughter following them. She didn't seem to mind woman's work but refused to put herself in the position of wife to anyone. She still begged to go on river trips with Pap. She daydreamed too much, and Mama had caught her many times at the river swimming in her underclothes, her dress neatly hung on a bush.

You seem a bright child, Mama thought. Is something wrong inside your head that we can't see?

Rachel danced a little jig on the way to the fence with more wash.

. . .

Rachel's heart beat faster and excitement welled up inside her. The buttermilk pie in her hands shook a little as she approached the house. Rachel didn't know what was wrong. She didn't feel afraid. Meeting new people never bothered her and she was always eager to make new friends and maybe hear their adventures.

A pleasant but tired looking woman answered her knock.

"Good morning. I'm your neighbor, Rachel, and I brought a pie to welcome you to Cincinnati." Rachel extended her gift.

A smile broadened on the woman's face.

"Please come in. I'm very glad to meet you." The thick Irish accent left no doubt as to where she was from.

Rachel was ushered into the house and into the kitchen where introductions were made.

"I'm Margaret, and this is my son, Edward. The Mister is already off to his new job and, as you can see, we have quite a bit of a job before us, getting everything unpacked and the house in order."

Rachel and Edward's eyes locked.

Margaret pulled a chair out from the table. "Sit down, Rachel. Tell us about your family, and this city we've moved into."

Rachel sat, but remained silent, and stared across the table at Edward. Who is this boy, she thought. I know him. His eyes . . . yes, I know him. Rachel felt her heart swell with love.

Edward looked at Rachel with a huge smile.

Margaret frowned, and took a seat at the table. "What kind of work does your father do?"

"He's . . . he's on the river."

"Is he a fisherman?"

"No. He just . . . goes in a boat."

"Is your mum at home?"

"Yes." Rachel hadn't looked away from Edward.

Margaret reached over and put her hand around Rachel's forearm. "I'll come over tomorrow to meet her, if that will be all right."

Rachel finally broke her gaze with Edward and looked at Margaret. "Yes, ma'am. That will be fine."

Margaret stood up. "Please don't think me rude, but I've got a lot of work to do. Tell your mum I'll be over tomorrow."

Rachel blinked her eyes and gave her head a small shake. "Yes ma'am. I'll tell her." She got up, walked through the house and out the door.

Margaret shook her head as she watched Rachel leave. "What a shame. A pretty girl like that, tetched in the head."

Edward remained silent and looked longingly after Rachel.

Rachel found herself back in her own house without much memory of exactly what happened. Mama spoke to her several times but she seemed to have difficulty understanding.

One of her daydreams again. Oh, Rachel, child. When are you going to wake up to the real world? Mama kept her thoughts to herself and left Rachel alone when she chose to settle under a tree in the back yard for the rest of the afternoon.

The guardians greeted each other joyfully.

Aspen grasped Willow's hand. "It's good to see you again, my friend. How is your Edward?"

Aspen and Willow floated quietly between the two houses, and caught up on all the happenings of the years they had been apart.

Edward knocked nervously on the door. When the woman opened it, he stuttered his greeting.

"H-h-hello. I'm Edward, y-y-your neighbor. Rachel said ... she said she'd show me around this afternoon."

"Come in, Edward. Rachel's in the back yard." She welcomed him in.

Poor boy, she thought as she led him through the house. The accent is bad enough, but he stutters too.

Rachel turned her head when they came out the back door. Without a word she rose, walked to Edward and took his hand. A perplexed frown furrowed Mama's forehead as the pair walked off toward the river still holding hands and still without a word being spoken. The eighteen-year-old woman and the twelve-year- old boy, looking as if they had always walked like this.

Edward and Rachel sat by the river facing each other, their eyes searched the others face, searched for understanding.

"Did you live in Ireland or New York?" Edward lost his stutter.

"No. I was born just a few miles from here." Rachel sighed and looked toward the water. "I know what you're talking about, but we couldn't have met before."

Edward finally broke into a large smile and reached for Rachel's hand again. "Well, we both have grand homes here by the Ohi and I know we'll be best friends." A deep sense of satisfaction settled through him. "Tell me everything about yourself. If we're going to be best friends, I'd better know who you are." He was happier than he could ever remember being.

"It's joyous to see them together again, but is the age difference going to be a problem?" Aspen said as he settled himself in a tree overlooking the couple.

Aspen watched the couple with a satisfied smile. "I don't understand it, but that's not part of our job. We never know what They have planned. Remember in our training They covered predestination and free will. I don't think I ever fully grasped it. The main thing They made me understand was that we are guardians and companions. We do what we can to keep them safe and happy but their free will is stronger than us."

Aspen moved his wings and fanned a slight breeze over the couple, cooling them on this extra warm day. "When Rachel is happy, I'm happy. Today is a very good day."

Rachel and Edward sat and talked until the lightning bugs began to twinkle in the evening dusk. The mothers' voices combined, calling them home for the supper hour. Reluctantly their hands parted as they neared the houses.

"Tomorrow?" Edward asked.

"Tomorrow." Rachel assured.

"I don't know what's got into the girl. All the nice young men that come around and she wants to spend all her time with that boy, a mere child. I'm truly starting to think there's something wrong in her head. Today she takes a pan and matches from the kitchen and says they're cooking fish by the river for dinner. She's playing like she was twelve." Mama bustled around the kitchen clearing away the supper dishes. That was Rachel's job, but Rachel had run out the door as soon as she finished eating. Edward had called from the yard.

Pap lit his pipe and leaned back in his chair.

"Maybe I should take her on my next trip. She's always begged to go and that would get her away from the boy for a spell."

Mama always objected to Rachel going on the boat trips, but now she stopped and gazed out the kitchen window.

"I think that might be a good idea," she said after a thoughtful moment. "Tell her tonight when she gets home."

***

The one thing she had always begged from her Pap was now being given to her. Her emotions jogged from one side to the other. To finally go down the river and see the things only heard of before. But she would have to leave Edward behind, and she wanted to spend every waking hour with him.

"How long do you think we would be gone?" Rachel bit her lower lip waiting for the answer. Sometimes Pap was gone only a week but other times he was gone for a month or more.

"This is a short trip. One week, maybe two at most. Well, do you want to go or not? That's all I've heard for years, and now you can't make up your mind?" Pap and Rachel sat on the front steps where Edward had reluctantly left her at dark.

"I guess I want to go," Rachel answered hesitantly. "When do we leave?"

"Day after tomorrow at dawn. Be ready. Better go over to one of your brother's tomorrow, and see about borrowing a pair of britches for yourself. Can't work a boat in one of those frilly dresses."

Rachel grinned. Going on the boat and getting to wear pants too. She was sure Edward would understand. He always understood what was in her mind and heart, and it would only be for a week or two.

"Rachel, I have a bad feeling about this. You and Edward are together again. Don't leave him, even for a short time." Aspen's pleas went unheeded. The lure of the long awaited boat trip was too strong.

"Thank you, Pap." Rachel jumped up and ran in the house calling, "Mama, guess what!"

***

Margaret put her arms around her son and held him close. They stood on the bank of the Ohio. The sky was overcast and gray, reflecting in the river. The water looked dark and ominous. Edward stared out at the river, but his mother's sad eyes were on him.

"You need to come to the house, Edward. Looking at the river isn't going to bring her back. It was just a bad accident and she's gone. I know she was your friend but it will serve no good purpose to make yourself sick over it. You haven't eaten a bite in two days, since the news of her drowning came, and I don't think you've slept either. The best thing for you to do is go talk to her mother and father, poor souls. If you're this heart sick, imagine what they must feel? But life must go on, yours and theirs, so pull yourself together and come to supper." Reluctantly, he allowed himself to be guided toward the house.

Life did go on in the blossoming new world, but Edward never seemed to take part in it. He never married, and died in 1854 in Kentucky when the coalmine where he worked had a cave-in. Twenty-three men were trapped in the deep shaft. The bodies were never recovered.

"Are you ready to go home now, Edward?" Willow sat by Edward's side. His soft glow pushed back the suffocating blackness that had descended when the last lamp went out.

"Sure, if you think you can get me out of here."

"All of you will get out now. Do you remember me?"

Edward's thoughts began to clear. He felt like he had been asleep a long time.

"Willow!" As all his memories returned, the next word was a whispered question. "Rachel?"

"She's waiting for you. Ready to go?"

"I've been ready for the past twelve years. What are we waiting for?"

All the guardians and their charges ascended, leaving the world and their mortal remains behind.

Chapter 3

1861

Rachel and Edward stood at the edge of the woods by the meadow. They laughed at two fawns that played while their mother looked on proudly.

Edward grew quiet and took Rachel's hand, but continued to gaze across the meadow. "It's time for me to go back. The woman who is to be my mother is ready."

"Oh, Edward. So soon? I hope I'm not far behind you. Do you think we could find out where you'll be?"

"You know They won't tell us that, but I know the couple are nice people. He has a physical deformity but they love each other very much. I'm sure they'll love and care for me, too. And it really doesn't matter where I'll be. You know we'll find each other somehow. Maybe this time we'll grow old together. Twice before we didn't listen to the prompting of our guardians, and the results were hard."

Rachel encircled Edward with her arms and put her head on his shoulder. "I pray for wisdom, and to choose the right path. The earthly world sometimes leads us where we shouldn't go." She raised her head and looked into his eyes. "I love you. Keep that in your heart, and look for me."

"Always, my precious, always."

***

25

"Damn, damn, damn!" Rose hissed the profanities through clenched teeth as she paced the kitchen floor. "If I had known this damn war was going to start, I'd never have gotten like this." She stopped pacing, bent slightly and grasped the edge of the cabinet. Another contraction started.

Charles sat at the table, his hands fidgeting on the wooden top.

"Please don't talk like that, Rose. Just think about how many years we hoped and prayed for a child. Now it's almost here. Don't you think you should lie down on the bed now?"

A crooked spine and one short leg had kept Charles home with his pregnant wife when others in the town left to join the Union army. His deformity was never a problem for them or shadowed the love between them. He pulled himself out of the chair and limped to her side. She leaned on him as he helped her into the next room.

"Mrs. Delaney will be here soon to help you through this. Everything will be all right. By this time tomorrow you'll be holding our baby."

"But why did the doctor have to up and leave town right now when I need him?"

"Rosie, honey, women have babies all the time without doctors. If we didn't live in a town you wouldn't even think about that. Our good doctor felt he would be needed to help the wounded fighting men. He told me he would use his skill to help anyone, on either side, hurt by this madness. I'm sure this war will be over soon and we can raise our child in a peaceful, safe world."

Charles helped Rose undress and slip into a loose nightgown. He settled her into the bed and brought extra pillows for her head. Every few minutes a moan escaped from her lips as the contractions became more frequent and harder.

She grabbed his hand. "I know I'm not being very brave about this. I've never been with anyone when they were having a baby. I went to see my friend, Ruth, three days after her baby was born, and she was up and dressed, acting like nothing was wrong. She didn't tell me it hurt this bad." She squeezed his hand hard and a sob escaped her lips as another contraction started. "How long is this going to go on?"

"I don't know, sweetheart. I don't know."

Mrs. Delaney arrived and scurried around, very much in charge. She gave orders and eased the minds of the couple with her confidence.

Willow settled softly into a corner of the room and smiled a greeting to the other three guardians. The wait would not be long. Edward would soon make another appearance on earth and begin a new life with much to learn.

***

"Are you certain you want to do this, Rachel? It may be a very hard life for you in that household." Aspen sat with Rachel in a foggy place. They could see nothing but each other.

"Of course I'm certain. There are so many injustices happening there. Surely this time I'll take some of my knowledge and love with me to help in my new life. Isn't that what all these return trips are about, learning to love and help more?"

Aspen looked down and breathed a silent prayer for forgiveness. With conditions on Earth as they were then, he knew this new life would be difficult. He knew also that the choice was hers to make. If this was the path to wisdom that she chose, this was the path she must take.

"You're right, and I'm glad you can see that. Forgive me. Guardians aren't always perfect, you know."

"Well, I think you're perfect," Rachel laughed. "Now, isn't it about time for us to leave?"

"Yes, my sweet rebel. Go now and I'll soon join you. Take care and don't try to change the whole world in one life time."

Aspen and Rachel embraced and parted.

***

Beth grew up on the plantation next to the one where she lived now. Her father was the overseer of that place just as her husband was the overseer of this one. As a child, she roamed the two farms and met Hattie in the fields one season when the cotton was being picked.

Hattie pulled a small cotton sack behind her and couldn't stop to play. Beth walked along beside her and talked. Beth's easy, friendly conversation finally dispelled Hattie's caution and the two spent many days talking in the hot, southern sun. The friendship deepened when Beth began to slip away from home at night to visit Hattie in the slave quarters of the adjoining farm. This made Hattie's parents nervous but they were in no position to tell a white child what she should and shouldn't do.

Beth was only a few weeks older than Hattie, but a good head taller. She wheedled her mother into letting her take her out-grown clothes to Hattie without her father's knowledge. Hattie became the best dressed child in the quarters. In the winter she possessed a warm wrap. She wore it proudly to the church services conducted by the old man known privately in the congregation as Chief. As the girls grew older, the size difference changed. Hattie took on the rotund figure of her mother, but the friendship between the girls remained the same.

The visits grew fewer as Hattie's workload increased and Beth attended school. At fourteen Hattie was married to an older man whose wife had died and left him with two children. At seventeen Beth married Clayton, the assistant overseer of Hattie's plantation. Three years later he became the overseer and Beth was expecting a child.

(1861)

Now the two friend's lives were in turmoil. A war had broken out that could mean monumental changes for them. The uncertainty of the future was frightening. Each publicly supported the cause of their own race when a group conversation with peers made it necessary. Privately they clung together and cried with fear. They treasured the few moments they could share together.

"Miss Beth, Miss Beth!" Hattie's frantic cries carried into the house as she rushed across the yard. Beulah, one of the big house servants, opened the back door for her when she reached it.

"She's fine," Beulah said as Hattie pushed by her. "She's in there in the bed with her new baby girl."

Hattie heard the words but didn't stop. She rushed on into the bedroom to kneel by Beth's side.

"Why didn't you send for me, Miss Beth? You knowed I would've come and helped." Hattie's dark, work worn hand brushed the hair back from Beth's pale forehead.

"Oh, Hattie. It all started happening so fast." She took Hattie's hand in her own and pressed it to her cheek. "And with everything going on like it is . . ." she paused and gazed into the loving eyes above her. "I really didn't know if your man would let you come."

Hattie laughed and the worry lines around her eyes relaxed a little.

She patted Beth's cheek. "Honey, you should know me good enough to know I can usually get around that man no matter what he say. Are you all right?"

"I'm fine now. Take a look at my beautiful Rachel."

Hattie got up and walked to the other side of the bed where the baby girl lay, and picked her up.

"Well, hello there, Miss Rachel. Ain't you a pretty little thing?" She cuddled the small bundle against her ample breasts. She loved Beth and would likewise love this baby.

In the quiet bedroom with the new baby between them, the moment was like gold.

Hattie placed Rachel back on the bed and got a fresh pan of water from the kitchen. She bathed Beth's face and hands and brushed her long hair.

"The big house servants don't know how to tend to people. Next time this happens, you better send for me." Hattie straightened the bed linens and pillows.

Beth chuckled. "Just between you and me, I hope it's a long time till the next time." The pain of the delivery was still fresh in her mind.

"I got to get on back to work now. I saw your Mr. Clayton going into the big house as I was coming across the yard but he'll be back to the fields soon. He and the Master has both been on a tear since this war thing started, and I don't care much to feel the lash like some of the others has. Now don't you stir from that bed. Make that lazy girl in there fetch for you. I'll be back to check on things first chance I get, when your Mister ain't here." Hattie bent to place a kiss on Beth's cheek and felt the wetness of tears.

"I'm so sorry, Hattie. If I could change anything, you know I would."

"Hush before you get Rachel upset. Babies can tell when the mamas is and start the colic." With a parting hug, Hattie left the house.

****

1865

"Charles, I'm so proud of you. Bank president! Doesn't that sound grand? Did you have any idea Mr. VanWort was going to offer you the job?" Rose couldn't be still. She talked and rushed about the kitchen, putting their supper on the table. Edward sat quietly in his high chair and watched the excited exchange between his parents.

"No idea at all. Of course I'd hoped but so did everyone at the bank. As soon as we heard there would be a branch opening in the south, everyone kind of polished up their work." Charles laughed, "I guess I was the best polisher."

"How soon will we be moving? Do I need to start packing right away?" Rose's tone of voice indicated she was ready to leave the dinner table and start boxing things up.

"You won't have to hurry. It will be at least six months to a year before things are ready. Mr. VanWort said we should let things calm down a little and, anyway, some work needs to be done on the building he bought for the bank. I'll probably go down in a couple of months to get the feel of the place and see how the work is progressing. I'll look around for a house too while I'm there. How are you going to like being a southern lady and the wife of a bank president?"

"Why, sir," Rose stopped and put one of the plates she carried in front of her face like a fan. She attempted a Southern accent drawl. "I think you'll find I can be just as refined as you need me to be."

Charles laughed uproariously. "I have no doubts, Rosie. No doubts. But keep that accent to yourself."

***

"Hattie, I'm so relieved we'll be in the same town. When you first told me you and your husband were leaving for the city, I was heartbroken and almost begged you to stay. Then Clayton comes in that same night and tells me we're moving too. When he said where, I know I looked crazy, laughing and hugging him. He couldn't understand and said he didn't know I wanted to leave so bad. Of course I couldn't tell him why. You know how he is."

Beth and Hattie sat on a quilt in a wooded area by one of the fields. Rachel lay on her stomach between them, idly trying to build a house with small twigs and leaves. She loved these times when Hattie and her mother were alone together. She could feel the deep affection that flowed between the women and onto her, wrapping her in contented love.

***

Hattie began cleaning off the breakfast table. She liked working for these people. Some of the whites in town talked about them behind their backs but couldn't openly show disdain for the family privately referred to as 'those carpet baggin' Yankees'. Mr. Charles was the president of the only bank in town and, with the struggling economy, he had to be dealt with. Miss Rose held her own in the small affluent group considered 'society'. She gave and received the invitations deemed necessary for one in her position.

Little Edward, however, was not so fortunate. The local children heard their parents talk and knew the true feelings most of the adults harbored for the newcomers. They shunned Edward and, when association was forced on them at parties and teas, were deliberately cruel. Edward, in his stoic manner, quietly withdrew from the other children and stayed by himself as much as possible.

"Miss Rose, you through with your breakfast now?" Hattie asked before removing the few remaining dishes.

Rose lifted the open newspaper she was reading from the empty plate before her. "Yes, of course, Hattie. I was just looking at all the new styles of clothes in this New York newspaper. Can't really see any point in ordering anything, though. I haven't worn all the new things I bought before we came down here."

"Yes, Ma'am, you sure got some nice things." Hattie hesitated by the table still holding the dirty dishes. "Miss Rose, could I ask a boon of you?"

"Certainly. Do you need some extra money for something?"

"No, Ma'am. There's this white lady I've known a long time and she be doing poorly carrying a baby. It's not coming for another three months. The doctor say she needs to stay in bed. That's gunna be hard to do cause she got a little girl same age as Mr. Edward. I was wondering if I could bring little Rachel with me every day for a while. That way Miss Beth could stay in bed and Mr. Edward would have a playmate." Hattie waited nervously for the answer.

"I think that would be a lovely idea." Rose folded the newspaper thoughtfully and laid it aside. "I worry about Edward being by himself so much. You just bring that little girl first thing in the morning. I know they'll have a wonderful time together. And I think it's very nice that you want to help this lady. Did you work for her?"

"Yes, Ma'am. Her husband was the overseer at the place I was 'til the war was over." Hattie saw no need to explain the long and unusual friendship between her and Beth.

"Well, isn't that something. I've heard some horrible stories about the way you Negroes were treated, but if you still want to help this lady, I guess we can't believe everything we hear."

"Yes, Ma'am." Hattie went on with her morning chores, relieved she could be of help to her beloved Beth.

Edward sat on his bed, head down and arms crossed. He didn't want to go down to breakfast. He didn't want to meet another child that would torment him as the others did. His mother stood in the open door.

"Edward, quit acting like a baby and come down to breakfast right now. We're all waiting at the table. Rachel is a very sweet girl and she's come to play with you."

With a resigned sigh, he slid off the bed and followed his mother to the dreaded meeting.

Rachel sat nervously at the table. This house was as fine as the big house at her old home, but she had never eaten in the big house. She watched the doorway for the first sight of the boy that was to be her new playmate.

Edward entered the room and took his usual seat without looking up.

"Edward, say good morning to Rachel," his father urged.

"Good morning." With those quiet words, Edward looked up directly at Rachel across the table. A smile slowly formed on his lips and spread into a large grin. "Hello, Rachel." The tone of his voice had suddenly changed.

Rose gave a relieved sigh. "That's better. Now you two eat your breakfast so you can go outside to play. It's a beautiful day."

The children hurried through the meal and left the table without asking to be excused. From the kitchen window, Hattie watched them run across the back yard and climb into the old magnolia tree.

"You climb trees good, Rachel. Most girls can't." Edward offered his hand as Rachel reached the branch he was on and helped her make the last step up.

"I like trees," Rachel replied shyly. "I like you too, Edward." The last words brought a blush to her fair cheeks.

Edward grinned and moved to swing by his legs from the branch they were on. He wanted to impress this beautiful creature.

Rachel gasped. "Be careful, Edward. You could fall."

Edward grinned, and hung there a moment longer. The legs of his pants had scooted up, and the bark cut painfully into the bare skin behind his knees. But he didn't want Rachel to see his discomfort.

"Easy there, boy." Willow held firmly to Edward's feet.

"I think we have our work cut out for us this time." Aspen guardedly put his arms on either side of Rachel in case she should lose her balance.

Willow slowly released Edward's feet as he returned to his seated position. "Yes, but it's wonderful to see them together again. That's the only time they're truly happy."

And thus, the soul mates began another life together.

1872

Tutoring time was over, and Edward and Rachel sat in their favorite place in the magnolia tree enjoying the cookies Hattie had given them.

"Edward, do you think we'll be happy when we're growed up?"

"Of course we will. Why do you ask that?"

Rachel shrugged and took another bite of cookie before answering. "Mama and Daddy aren't happy. Daddy complains about his work all the time, and Mama stays tired from taking care of little Clay. He's sick every day and most nights. They argue a lot, too. Does your Mama and Daddy ever argue?"

"No," Edward answered with a snorted laugh. "What do they have to argue about?"

"I don't know." Rachel smiled. "Maybe we won't have to argue either." Then she turned her attention to the remaining cookies.

The last seven years life had been almost perfect for Rachel and Edward. They spent six days a week together. Rachel came with Hattie each morning and stayed until the workday was over. Sunday was a day to be endured alone. Edward's parents took him to church, and Rachel just tried to stay out of her father's way. Clayton usually chose Sunday to drink and had no patience with little Clay who cried a lot, and little patience with Rachel. Little Clay demanded all of his mother's attention.

When Edward and Rachel reached school age, Edward refused to attend public school and Charles hired a tutor to come to the house. At Edward's insistence, Rachel was included in these lessons and both pleased the tutor greatly with their desire to learn. The closeness of the children was noted and approved of by Edward's parents. With Rachel's parents, Clayton was unaware and didn't care where his daughter attended school. Beth was just thankful Hattie saw to Rachel and took that responsibility off her tired life.

"I'm glad Rachel has this time of childhood with Edward. Her life at home isn't very pleasant." Aspen shared this thought with Willow as they sat in the tree with the children.

"Have you spoken with Clayton's guardian about this?" Willow asked.

"Several times but he seems unable to get through to Clayton. Especially when he's drinking. I fear Clayton's free will may cause some hard times for Rachel in the near future.

"Clayton, you can't be serious about this. We have a comfortable life here. Little Clay is too sick to travel. Much less travel as far as you're talking about. And in a wagon train? For once in your life, try thinking about someone other than yourself." Beth tried to remain calm but the unshakable plans of her husband brought a desperate sound to her voice.

Clayton leaned close to her and sneered. "I think it's time you took that advice."

She could smell the alcohol as each word spat from his mouth.

"You should think about your husband some instead of spending all your time with that sick whelp you call a son. You know I hate this god-damned town. Have always hated it. I hate working with them lazy niggers. I can't even lay a strap to 'em because I'm not the boss. Now I've got a chance to go where I am the boss, my own boss. There's plenty of land and we won't have a neighbor so close we can smell his toilet. You got a week to get everything packed you want to take because that's when we're leaving. There'll be no more talk about it." Clayton turned his back on his sobbing wife, and raised the bottle for another swallow. He glanced back at her. "You do what I say." Then he left the house.

Clayton had not gone to his town job all week. Instead, he used that time to dispose of household items and outfit a wagon. A day away from leaving found him inside at the breakfast table.

Hattie and Beth spoke with whispered words outside the house. The two women talked every chance they could, consoling each other and crying until no more tears came. Rachel stood close and watched the exchange with wide-eyed fright.

"You leaving in the morning for sure?" Hattie asked. She was close to tears.

"That's what Clayton says. We have to finish packing the wagon today. Hattie, I feel like I'm breaking into little pieces inside." Beth threw her arms around her friend, not caring who saw.

"You know I'd do something if I could, Miss Beth." Her habit of using the title had not ended with her emancipation. "You been in my life so long, I can't even see what it will be like without you. But all us women be slaves, Honey, no matter what the president say. When our men tells us to do, we do, and when they says go, we go. Always been like that."

Beth pulled away from Hattie and tried to compose herself. "You're sure Rose won't mind me sending letters to her house for you?"

"She don't mind a bit and said she'd read them to me."

Rachel could no longer think about this horrible thing that was happening. The idea of life without Edward or Hattie was more than she could bear. She clutched her mother as though she could keep the two of them there.

***

"Edward, I'm so scared. I don't know where Daddy's taking us. It must be somewhere very far away. I may never see you again."

Rachel's words were muffled. She buried her face in the pillow on Edward's bed. She had been crying almost from the minute the two children had gone into Edward's room. It was Saturday and the tutor wasn't there.

"I know. I tried to get Mother and Father to talk to your parents about letting you stay here with us but they just say a child should be with their parents. They don't understand." Edward sat by Rachel, stoking her hair, his young heart breaking. His life had been so perfect with Rachel. The thought of life without Rachel left him numb and frightened.

"Remember our plan." Edward made Rachel set up and held her by the shoulders, looking deep into her eyes. "You will write and tell me where you are and as soon as we are old enough, I'll come get you. Promise you'll remember."

"I promise." Rachel dissolved into tears again, this time joined by Edward. They clung together feeling lost in the adult world where they had no say in their own lives.

Aspen and Willow hovered close. The pain and love they felt for their charges was beyond human understanding. Their only consolation was prayer.

The dust, heat, and hardship of the miles were unending. Little Clay died three weeks into the journey. Clayton would have buried him at the campsite, but the other members of the train expressed their sympathy for Beth, and carried the body two more days. When they reached a settlement with a church and graveyard, they laid the small body to rest.

Beth lost herself somewhere during that time and was with the group in body only. Rachel cared for her mother and tried to assume the chores for their small family. Clayton was unappreciative of her efforts and more than once lashed out physically when the childish attempts did not meet his expectations. He sat sometimes and stared at Beth. Rachel could see the hate in his eyes. The miles continued to grow between Rachel and the happiness she had known.

***

The three Indian scouts lay in concealment on top of the bluff watching the wagon train pass below them. A few weeks earlier another wagon train had passed, also unaware of the watching eyes. Days later the Indians found the buffalo herd they hunted slaughtered. The wagon train had been buffalo hunters who took the skins and tongues and left the carcasses to rot. This would not happen again.

Early the next morning the sky was pink as if a prediction of the bloody earth it would soon look down on. The attack was swift and merciless.

All the guardians of both sides withdrew and turned their back on the carnage. Some things angels can't endure to watch.

The promised letters to Edward and Hattie never came.

Edward grew to maturity and followed his father into banking. In his late thirties he married a woman equal to his social station, and endured almost twenty years of a loveless, childless marriage. Death in his fifties was welcomed and he could once again find happiness with Rachel, his soul mate.

Chapter 4

1920

Edward and Rachel held hands as they wandered through a beautiful pine forest. Bird songs echoed around them in the strange way sounds seem to carry in woods like these. Each step brought the tangy smell of crushed pine needles. Aspen and Willow followed at a discreet distance. All four enjoyed exploring the many faceted locations provided for them and all the others that resided at this plane of existence.

Rachel plucked a small branch from a low hanging limb and inhaled the fresh fragrance. She held it up to Edward and smiled as he breathed deeply, her own enjoyment magnified with the sharing.

"My class this morning was especially good," Rachel said. "It seems I have a lot more to learn about self-assurance and impatience."

Edward took the branch from her and idly brushed the soft needles against his cheek.

"Mine covered more of the basics. They stressed the part about letting my conscience be my guide. I've got a strong feeling They were trying to prepare me for the next trip back."

"Let's not think about that now," Rachel said. "I just want to enjoy the here and now."

Rachel stopped and pulled Edward to the side of the path. A spider slowly weaved a web between two close tree trunks. They watched in silence as the beautiful, intricate creation took form.

Chicago

"Do any of you guys know where Smitty is?" Hildi asked from the doorway.

The four men around the table ignored her. The cards and money on the table took all their attention.

Hildi stepped further into the room and raised her voice. "Lewis, where is Smitty?"

Lewis didn't look up from his cards. "Damn, Hildi. Can't you see we're busy. Smitty left an hour ago. You know he had that shipment to pick up tonight."

"I guess one of you have to do it then." Hildi turned back into the doorway and leaned against it.

Lewis carefully removed two cards from his hand and put them face down on the table. "Do what?"

"Take me to the hospital. This kid is trying to come out." Hildi straightened as the contraction passed.

Lewis picked up the two cards the dealer had slapped on the table in front of him. "Now? Can't you wait? These cards are hot."

Groans and curses came from the other three at the table as they threw their cards down. "I'm out," circled the table.

"See what you done!" Lewis pushed his chair back and threw his own cards down. "I could've got back some of my money with that hand, maybe all of it." He abruptly stood up, knocking his chair over. "Let's go, then, and get this stinking kid taken care of. Maybe they won't cool off before I get back."

Lewis stomped from the room but as soon as he was out of the sight of his poker partners, his attitude changed. He took the paper bag Hildi carried, held her arm, and carefully guided her out the door and down the steps. He opened the car door and helped her in as if she were made of fine china.

Willow divided his attention between Hildi in the cold white room and Lewis in the smoky waiting room. The conflicting impressions Lewis gave between his words and actions intrigued Willow. Lewis didn't leave Hildi at the hospital and return to his cronies. For a while he would sit on the edge of a chair in the waiting area. Then he would jump up, pace the well-worn floor, and light a cigarette from the butt of the last one.

Willow approached Lewis's guardian to question him about the curious behavior.

"I'm Willow, guardian to the one being born."

"I'm Milkweed. I thought that's probably who you were."

"Your charge confuses me. He seemed so different earlier at their house. He talked gruff and uncaring. Now it looks as if he truly cares about the outcome of this birth."

Milkweed chuckled. "Yeah, that's Lewis, all right. He'd rather get shot than let the other guys know how he feels. He loves Hildi, has loved her for years. But there's a big problem. Smitty is his best friend. They grew up together and were friends for years before Hildi came along. He knows it wouldn't be right to let his feelings show."

Willow studied Lewis for a moment with new understanding and respect. "That's very commendable. You must be proud of him."

"I am. He has a heart of gold." Milkweed looked at Lewis with a slight frown. "Well, maybe only silver, and a little tarnished. But basically, he's a very good man."

Willow returned to Hildi's side when it became obvious Edward was almost there. A lusty cry brought a smile to Willow's face. The miracle of birth had started Edward's life again and the wonder of it was a thing of indescribably beauty.

Missouri

"Pray, Mary! Pray for forgiveness of your sins and the sins of Eve that make it necessary for you to suffer this pain." Reverend Horace stood at the foot of the bed and glared at his wife, scornful of her outcries.

Tears ran down Mary's pale face and pleading showed in her eyes.

"I'm sorry Horace. Please forgive my weakness." Mary grabbed the iron rails at the head of the bed as another contraction brought a scream from her lips. "Forgive me. Oh, God, forgive me!"

Three women in the room knelt to one side, praying earnestly and loudly. The fourth sat in a chair beside the bed and bathed Mary's face with a damp cloth. She occasionally raised the covers to check the progression of the pending birth. The four were members of Reverend Horace's small congregation.

Another outcry from Mary brought a sheen of sweat to Horace's face and he paled. He backed away from the bed.

"I'll continue praying in the other room. What remains in here is women's work." He turned, left the room, and quickly closed the door behind him.

A look of disgust from the woman by the bed followed Horace.

"Men. They're anxious enough to get us in this condition for their pleasure, but they sure don't want to stay around when the pleasure brings the pain." She softly bathed Mary's face again. "It's almost over, Dear. You scream all you want to."

Aspen exchanged looks of concern with the other guardians in the room. All of the glows were subdued. The fear, tension, pain, and even some hatred felt by the humans in the room were reflected in their guardians.

Aspen knew Horace believed his strict ways were right. His harsh treatment of Mary was much different from what Aspen had been taught was the right way people should treat each other. Horace sincerely believed women were secondary in God's eyes and could only receive grace through the intervention of men. It was a man's place to keep the woman in his life from committing sins that the worldly life put in her path every day.

Aspen felt compassion and love for sweet, submissive Mary and rejoiced when Rachel finally arrived to start her new life in this troubled family. Hopefully her presence would bring some happiness and a little more tolerance.

Hildi rocked slowly as she held Edward. She frowned with concern when she felt of his face and noted the heat and slight flush.

"I don't think I'll go with you tonight, Smitty. He's got a fever and I'd better stay here and watch him."

Smitty left the table where he was cleaning and loading a revolver. He crossed the room to feel his son's forehead.

"He feels hot, all right. If he gets any worse, have Lewis take you to the hospital. You know I have to go. I'm the only one this bunch knows so they won't turn the load over to Burt. This is the biggest shipment we've gotten in a while and it's some of Canada's best ... a hundred and twenty proof." He returned to the table where Lewis, Burt and two others sat. He finished loading the gun and settled it into his shoulder holster.

When everything was ready, Smitty gave Hildi a brief goodbye kiss and bent lower to touch his lips to Edward's warm face.

Hildi grabbed his arm before he could walk away.

"Smitty, be extra careful tonight. The Feds seem to be working that part of the shoreline pretty heavy. Last time I went we were lucky we saw them before they saw us."

Smitty grinned broadly and winked. "Don't worry, Baby. I'm smarter than all the Feds put together."

He assured everyone he and Burt would be back before dawn, and they left.

Dawn came but Smitty and Burt did not return. Four hours later, a phone call from a friendly local policeman gave them the news. Smitty and Burt were dead, killed in a shoot-out with Federal agents. The shipment was confiscated and destroyed.

The funerals were quiet affairs with few attending. Everyone knew the Feds would be watching to see who paid their last respects. Fellow bootleggers made phone calls to Hildi and sent flowers and cards to the house. The clients Smitty delivered the illegal liquor to did nothing except search quickly for another source of merchandise.

Edward was too young to understand or care about the happenings. There were still three men in the house to give him attention and they more than made up for the two that were missing. Especially Lewis.

A month after Smitty and Burt were buried, Lewis moved his things into the bedroom shared by Hildi and Edward. Life went on as usual.

Horace stood behind the pulpit and looked out at the eighteen souls of his congregation. Attendance had dropped drastically in the three years he had been here. His sermons that stressed male dominance and female obedience had sharply decreased the number of female members in attendance. The majority of those before him now were men.

"My brothers and sisters. I have news that is both sad and joyous. It is sad that I must leave you, but the Lord has called me to another place where sin is rampant and His word is needed. The city of Chicago crawls with the evil of demon liquor. So with joy I go to do His will. I, along with my wife Mary and daughter Rachel, will miss the many friends and fellow Christians we have here. The last three years have been a true blessing. You have given us your love; sheltered, fed and clothed us. When you give your love offering today, please keep in mind the travel expense before us, and the uncertainty of the conditions we will find in Chicago. Search your hearts and keep in mind that the bread you cast upon the water to help do God's work will return to you tenfold. Now turn in your Bibles to Genesis 19 and we will read about the disobedience of Lot's wife and the horrible consequences it brought her."

The love offering was sufficient for the trip. The congregation had been generous. Most of the women emptied the last penny from their purses with mixed feelings of guilt and elation.

1933

As the years passed after Smitty's death, Edward slowly lost the name of Little Smitty. It was replaced with Eddie but he sometimes reverted to Smitty when he wanted to impress someone with his maturity. At fourteen he dropped out of school. At fifteen he was an established member of his mother's and Lewis's bootleg operation.

"Eddie, try on these new boots Lewis bought you."

Hildi picked up the boots beside her on the couch and handed them to him.

Edward sat by Hildi and pulled the boots on. The tops were extra big and would easily conceal the pints of liquor he delivered to private homes.

"Yeah, these fit swell. Do we have any deliveries for this afternoon?" He walked across the floor, getting the feel of the new boots.

Hildi went to the table and looked at the names and addresses on a piece of paper. "Yes, a few. You better take care of them early. There's a big order to be delivered tonight by truck. Want to eat before you go? I made a big pot of soup."

"Sure, Mom. That sounds good." Edward planted a loud kiss on his mother's cheek before he sat down at the table.

"Oh, Eddie." Hildi laughed and playfully hit Edward on the shoulder. "You're a scoundrel."

The love between the two was obvious. In this odd, mixed up household, Edward had always found love. Lewis more than filled the role of Father, and at an early age, Edward easily fell into the habit of calling him Pops. The other men that came and went in the business dealings were all congenial and friendly. Although the federal government might think of this group as disdainful and their activities illegal, Hildi, Edward and Lewis were happy with their lives and each other.

The only shadow that entered their conversations now was talk of a possible repeal of prohibition. Stories of the convention being convened dominated the newspaper headlines. A new government program being talked about was also in the news. The Work Progress Administration, or WPA, promised jobs for thousands of men.

Lewis assured Hildi he would take care of her and Eddie, no matter what the outcome of the convention. A hard working man could always find a job.

***

The only reading material allowed in the house was the Bible. Rachel sat at the kitchen table, totally absorbed in a forbidden magazine.

Horace was out for the evening, doing his nightly visitation, a job he felt was essential to keep his small and ever changing congregation on the straight and narrow. He loudly decried the work of the Devil when new members, drawn in by his enthusiastic charisma, stopped coming after a few weeks. He could not and would not accept the idea that his sermons belittling women had anything to do with the constant turnover of members. Once Mary suggested to Horace that such sermons might discourage married couples from attending, since women were often the ones that chose the church the family attended. Her reward was a hard slap and an order to scrub all the floors that had already been done that same day.

Rachel feared her father as much as Mary did but, at fifteen, found it hard to suppress her youthful curiosity about the world around her.

Her best friend, Margie, had secreted the magazine to her a few days before. She brought it out from the hiding place under her bed only when Horace was away from the house.

Mary was frightened for Rachel's disobedience but understood her daughter's longing to be like other girls. She smiled sadly at Rachel from the kitchen sink where she washed the dinner dishes.

"You should put that up now. Your father will be home soon." Mary poured the pan of wash water down the sink.

She was thankful Horace allowed her to use the running water in the house. He didn't let them use the electric lights. Rachel read the magazine by the light of a kerosene lamp. He also insisted all the cooking and heating of water be done on a wood burning stove. Modern conveniences led to idle time, time when the Devil could corrupt weak women.

Rachel lingered over one particular page picturing a beautiful model in a stylish dress and a short hair-do. She sighed.

"Mama, do you think father will ever let me get my hair cut?"

Mary left the sink and looked over Rachel's shoulder.

"No, baby. And don't get any ideas about dresses like that either. You know what your father thinks about being in style. Keep that in mind when you start looking for a man to marry."

Mary couldn't bring herself to say out loud what she was thinking. *Don't marry a man like your father.* "What's on the next page?" she asked.

"Harlots!" Horace glared at them from the kitchen door.

His angry shout drained the color from Mary and Rachel's faces. They cowered as his long strides brought him to the table.

"Must I watch you both every minute?" His voice pounded their ears as it did from the pulpit. "You defile this very house with the Devil's book instead of reading the word of God."

Horace snatched the magazine from the table and threw it violently into the stove. The embers from the evening meal flamed up with the added fuel.

"Father, that didn't belong to me. It's Margie's. Now I'll have to buy her another one." Tears welled up in Rachel's eyes.

Mary stepped in front of Rachel and tried to protect her. With a roar of rage, Horace pushed Mary to the floor. He raised his arm high and struck Rachel so hard it knocked her from the chair. He bent over Rachel's huddled form, his face purple with fury.

"I chastise you in the name of God," he hissed. "Go to your room. Don't leave it 'til you have prayed for and received forgiveness." He thrust his pointed finger within an inch of her face. "And I will tell you when you have received it."

Rachel quickly scooted backward on the floor, stumbled as she stood up from that awkward position, and ran to her room.

Horace then turned on Mary, rising up from the floor. He slapped her again, knocking her back to the floor. He grabbed the collar of her dress and pulled her to a sitting position. Twice more he slapped her, knocking her head from one side to the other.

"You have sinned doubly tonight. Not only did you look upon the devil's work but you allowed my daughter to see it too. Your punishment will be greater. Go to your bed. I must pray and ask for guidance."

Horace walked back to the living room with a purposeful stride. He sat in his chair by the front window, lit the lamp on the table beside him and picked up his Bible. He had once explained to Mary he read his Bible by the window so anyone walking by on the street would see him and feel ashamed that they weren't at home reading the Word Of God.

Mary stood up and braced herself against the sink. After a few moments, she wet a cup towel and pressed it to her stinging face. She blew out the lamp and slowly went to their bedroom. The darkness of the kitchen would never match the darkness of the feelings that hung over the house. There would be bruises the next day that showed, but the bruises in Mary's heart were much worse.

Rachel had shut her bedroom door quietly even though she longed to slam it as hard as she could. She lay on her bed and tears of anger ran down her face. She hated her father and his god. She felt the frustration of a trapped animal. She did pray. She prayed for freedom and release from the cruelty that dominated her life.

Rachel didn't know she had drifted off to sleep until the soft, persistent knock on her window woke her. She crawled quietly from her bed and looked at the door to be sure it was still closed before she crept to the window and opened it. Margie was there.

"Come on, Rach. Let's go have some fun," Margie whispered.

"Wait a minute." Rachel softly opened her bedroom door. The living room was dark and quiet. She carefully closed the door again, returned to the window and climbed out.

The two girls cautiously crept across the yard. Once at the street, they ran a block before stopping. They leaned against a building at the corner and giggled, breathless from the run. The corner streetlight circled them with light.

When they were finally able to control their laughter, Margie cupped Rachel's chin in her hand and turned her face toward the light. "You look like hell, Rach. Your old man been beating you again?"

"He found your magazine and burned it. I hate him!" Rachel pushed Margie's hand from her face and turned away from the light in shame and anger.

"Poo, it was just an old magazine, last month's issue. Let's go to my house and fix you up a little before we do anything else. The folks went to a new speakeasy in town so they'll be gone 'til late." Margie took Rachel's hand and they hurried on to her house.

Edward made his afternoon deliveries. He approached each house with a basket of vegetables, seeming to be a door-to-door peddler. Some answered his knock with obvious pleasure, handed him money, and took the bottle he pulled from the top of his boot with open smiles.

Others pulled him into the house furtively, and looked right and left to see if any neighbors watched the transaction.

When he returned home, he and Lewis loaded the pickup truck for the night delivery. They had more of Hildi's soup for dinner and the three of them played cards around the table until it was time to leave.

Lewis let Edward drive, directing him to an alley behind the new club that had just opened. The alley was clean and partially lit by the street light at the end.

"Stay here and watch the merchandise while I check things out," Lewis instructed.

Edward got out, leaned against the back of the truck, and watched the pedestrian traffic on the street. Two girls stopped at the edge of the alley. They smiled at him and whispered and giggled to each other.

Edward rested one foot behind him on the truck bumper and casually lit a cigarette. He didn't really like cigarettes but he thought smoking made him look older. He appraised the girls. Both were cute.

Margie had done a good make-over on Rachel. Makeup covered the red and slightly swollen cheek. Rachel's long hair was arranged on top of her head like older women sometime wore theirs. One of Margie's dresses and a little lipstick completed the transformation.

"I think this is the place the folks are at," Margie said. "Look at the boxes on that truck. Bet it's liquor. Isn't that guy by the truck cute?"

Edward took his foot from the truck bumper and strolled toward them.

"Hi, girls. Going to the new club?" He expertly flipped the cigarette into the street.

"We might. Haven't made up our minds yet." Margie leaned against the lamppost in a nonchalant manner.

Rachel was too nervous to say a word but she studied Edward closely until he looked directly at her. She dropped her eyes and wondered if the makeup hid the blush she felt creeping up her face.

"Don't I know you from somewhere?" Edward asked Rachel.

Margie poked Rachel in the side with her elbow. "You know this guy?"

Rachel looked up again and a queer feeling of recognition went through her.

"I – I don't know. Maybe." This time she let her gaze stay on Edward and a slight smile curved her lips.

He took Rachel's hand. "I'm Edward. What's your name?"

"Rachel." No more words would come. Emotions flooded through Rachel and she wanted to hold his hand forever.

"I'm Margie." She extended her hand but Edward didn't take his eyes off Rachel or acknowledge Margie's hand.

"Listen," Edward said. "uh . . ., I'll be through for the night as soon as we unload. Can you just hang around till then so we can talk?" He continued to hold Rachel's hand.

"Sure." Rachel saw Margie's astonished look.

Lewis came out the back door and motioned for Edward. Edward slowly released Rachel's hand and walked back to the truck.

Margie grabbed Rachel's arm and dragged her around the corner of the building, out of sight of the alley.

"Rach, I can't believe you. If you aren't something. That guy's really gone on you. Are you going to stay here and talk to him?" Margie's voice bubbled with excitement and giggles.

"Yeah, I guess so. You'll stay with me, won't you?" Common sense started coming back into Rachel's head. She still felt a little dazed and couldn't understand her own actions.

"Sure, I'll stay until you two love birds tell me to get lost. Maybe he has a friend that's as cute as him."

The two girls returned to the front of the alley and watched Edward and Lewis unload the boxes from the truck and carry them into the building.

Aspen and Willow touched wing tips. They hovered close to the street light which seemed to give off more light than the others on that street.

Willow's glow of exuberance was especially bright. "I was beginning to wonder if we'd be able to get these two together this time. They're in the same town but their families are worlds apart." He spread his wings apart as far as possible to demonstrate the distance between Edward's and Rachel's parents.

Aspen smiled in agreement. "It took the help of several other guardians to pull this off. But everyone is happy to help soul mates. Edward appears to be healthy and happy. I can't say the same for Rachel. Her life is hard. Horace's guardian is almost to the point of just leaving him. He's had several meetings with Them trying to straighten out that man's thinking."

Edward and Lewis unloaded the truck quickly. They left the building after the last boxes had been carried in, and Edward pulled Lewis to the front of the truck. He whispered to him for several minutes.

Lewis looked back at the two girls standing at the entrance to the alley and smiled.

"OK, kid, but don't stay out too late. You know your mother will worry herself sick if you do. And remember to act like a gentleman. These two girls look like fine young ladies to me so watch your manners and your mouth."

Rachel and Margie heard this exchange and grinned at each other.

Lewis got in the driver's side of the truck and Edward shut the door for him. He stood with his hands on the open window.

"I will, Pops, and I won't be too late. Thanks."

Edward stepped back from the truck and lifted one hand in a wave as Lewis backed out of the alley.

Lewis backed slowly past the girls and nodded his head at them. "Good evening, ladies."

Margie giggled, "Good evening to you, sir."

Rachel ducked her head and her blush returned.

Edward walked to the girls and again took Rachel's hand. "I know where there's a swell place. Have you been to the park a couple of blocks from here? There's a store just across the street from it where we can get sodas and benches in the park where we can talk."

The three headed in the direction of the park, with Edward holding Rachel's hand as if he never intended to let it go.

"We've got our work cut out for us," Aspen told Willow. "I'll speak to Horace and Mary's guardians. Horace's guardian will have to keep Horace in a deep sleep at night so Rachel can slip out to meet Edward. Mary's guardian must try to give her a sense of peace and understanding if she catches Rachel going out the window for one of the meetings. Her guardian will also have to allay any feelings of guilt, and get through to her she's not to tell Horace."

Willow nodded his head in agreement. "And I need to keep Edward safe. The work he does can be dangerous. I hope that changes soon."

The first few meetings took place in the park with Margie present. Soon Rachel was going by herself. She wore her plain, high neck, long sleeve dresses and no makeup. That didn't matter to Edward. He loved

Rachel just the way she was, and Rachel made it obvious she returned that love.

One night, after three weeks of park meetings, Edward took Rachel's hand and smiled his usual big smile.

"We're going to my house tonight. Mom and Pops want to meet you."

Rachel pulled her hand from his and stepped back. "Meet your parents? I don't know, Edward. Can't we . . . can't we just keep meeting here in the park?"

"Don't worry." Edward took her hand again. "They're swell. You'll like them."

When they got to Edward's home Hildi welcomed Rachel with a hug and Lewis beamed a broad smile when he shook her hand. A vase of fresh flowers sat in the middle of the table. To one side of the flowers was a cake, freshly made for the occasion. This was the first time Edward had brought a girl home to meet them. He knew Hildi had gone to extra effort to make the visit special.

The casual, friendly conversation soon had Rachel relaxed and enjoying herself. They sat around the table as Hildi served slices of cake with glasses of cold milk.

After the refreshments were finished and the dishes removed from the table, Edward cleared his throat. "Mom, isn't there something you need Pops to help you do in the kitchen?"

Hildi grinned. "Why, yes. Yes there is. Come on Lewis."

Lewis looked perplexed. "What do you need my help for?"

Hildi rolled her eyes up and sighed. "Just come on. I'll tell you in the kitchen."

Understanding suddenly flashed across Lewis's face and he jumped up from the table. "Sure, sure. We need to take care of that right away." Lewis followed Hildi into the kitchen. He turned and gave Edward a quick grin before he closed the door behind them.

Edward led Rachel to the couch and they sat close together. He put his arm around her and she turned toward him. The kiss was awkward and a little timid but effective.

"Rachel, I've never had a girlfriend before but I knew the minute I saw you that you were my girl. Do you feel that way about me?"

Rachel lost all her bashfulness and timidity. She placed her hands on each side of Edward's face and drew him back for another kiss, this one not so awkward.

"I love you, Edward. I think I've always loved you. These last few weeks have been the happiest time in my life. They've been the only happy times in my life. I want to stay with you and never have to go back to my father." Tears filled Rachel's eyes and spilled down her cheeks.

The two young lovers clung tightly to each other. Rachel cried openly on Edward's shoulder and Edward fought to control the tears that gathered in his eyes. He gently moved Rachel away from his shoulder and looked into her eyes. He clumsily tried to wipe the wetness from her face.

"You can stay here with me. Mom and pops know how mean your father is. I told them. They'll let you stay and keep him from hurting you any more." Edward longed to protect Rachel.

Rachel used the sleeve of her dress to wipe away the wetness that Edward had only spread across her face in his attempt to dry the tears.

"I know father would find me. I don't want to get you or your family in trouble. You don't know how he is when it comes to mother or me. I don't know what he'd do but it would be bad. No, I'll have to stay at home 'til I'm at least grown. Even then I don't think he'll be willing to let me leave."

Edward thought for a minute. "Then we'll run away, somewhere he'll never find you. I have enough money to get us a long way from here." Edward began to get excited as the plan formed in his mind. "Saturday night Mom and Pops are going to play cards with friends. I heard them talking about it. The people live just down the street so they'll walk and leave the truck here. I'll leave Mom and Pops a note and they'll understand. Then we can write them when we find a safe place to live. It'll work, Rachel. We're old enough to take care of ourselves so let's do it. Meet me in the park Saturday night, over by the benches just across the street from the store."

Fear muffled the hope building inside Rachel. *Could it be any worse than it is now? Can I really defy father? This means I have to leave mother. What would he do to me if he caught me leaving?* A hard core of determination began to form in her chest. Mother had told her to find someone different from Father. Well, she had found him.

"I love you, Edward, and I'll be at the park Saturday night, no matter what happens."

***

Saturday morning dawned without the sun. Low dark clouds blanketed the city. Rachel tried to keep her mood as somber as the weather and hid the excitement that bubbled inside her. Fear was also there, but desperation kept that in check. Her quiet docile attitude made Horace happy.

Shortly after noon the rain began. The light sprinkle soon turned into a steady drizzle that showed no sign of letting up.

Rachel and her mother worked quietly but steadily, doing all the Saturday chores. Horace sat at the kitchen table, his Bible and papers spread out before him as he worked on his Sunday sermon. Occasionally he would stop and look out the back door at the rain and talk to himself, rehearsing some phrase or sentence.

After the evening meal Horace settled into his usual chair by the window, lit the lamp and opened his Bible. Mary brought her knitting from the bedroom. She was working on a sweater for Rachel. Rachel picked up her Bible from the table by Horace. She held it close to her chest, and hoped he didn't notice her hands shaking.

"I'm going to read in my room." She bent and lightly kissed her father's cheek. "Goodnight." The thought of Judas kissing Jesus ran through her mind but she quickly dismissed it.

Rachel then went to her mother who sat quietly knitting, and stood for a few moments looking down at her. Her mother looked up and smiled. Rachel bent and hugged Mary fiercely with one arm, burying her face against Mary's neck.

"I love you," Rachel whispered before she stood up.

"I love you, too."

Rachel went to her room. Mary looked after her with a questioning, thoughtful look on her face.

Horace watched Rachel leave with a smug smile. He looked at his wife and his smile changed to a look of scorn. "You tell me I'm too hard on her but you can see what discipline and the word of God can do. She will become a decent, Christian woman. No daughter of mine can be anything else."

Aspen hovered by the door momentarily, exchanging looks with Horace's guardian. They knew Rachel's plan and had prayed it was the right thing to do. Mary's guardian looked sadly at her charge. Losing Rachel from her life would be the hardest thing Mary ever had to endure.

Rachel's sweaty hands trembled, and she had difficulty lighting the lamp by her bed. She sat on her bed and clutched the Bible. Her father's voice could be heard through the closed door but she couldn't make out the words. To calm her fears, she began to mentally list the things she would take.

This is one time I'm glad father never let mother or me have much. I can get all my clothes and things into one pillowcase.

When her nerves had settled slightly and her hands no longer shook, Rachel slipped her nightgown over her clothes. She took her shoes off, placed them at the edge of the bed and got under the covers. After what seemed like an eternity, she heard her parents stirring in the living room and knew they were preparing for bed. She opened the Bible and placed it on her chest as if she had fallen asleep while reading. Her eyes were closed when she heard the bedroom door open.

Mary tiptoed into the room, picked up the Bible and put it on the table by the bed. Rachel let her eyes flutter open when she felt her mother's lips on her forehead.

"Goodnight, Dear," Mary whispered and brushed Rachel's hair from her forehead.

"Goodnight, Mother," Rachel mumbled as she turned on her side. She glimpsed her father standing in the door before her mother blew out the lamp.

The thought of leaving her mother tore at her heart and she felt a panic of doubt. Hatred for her father over-shadowed her doubt. *I will leave.*

***

Rachel and her pillowcase of belongings were both soaked by the time she reached the park. She had run all the way, expecting to hear her father behind her with each step. A clump of bushes close to the street offered a safe, dark, wet hiding place where she could wait and watch for Edward. The street was deserted. The late hour and rain discouraged motorists from venturing out.

Headlights appeared around a corner, and Rachel held her breath. When she was sure it was Edward's truck, she exhaled deeply and stepped from the bushes. The truck stopped and the passenger door opened. She dashed across the small strip of ground and threw herself into the cab of the truck.

Edward gathered her trembling form into his arms.

"Are you all right?"

"Yes. Just wet and scared. Let's leave now, please, before father catches me." Rachel shut the truck door that she had left open in her haste.

Edward put the truck in gear and pulled out into the street. He had no definite destination ... just far away from this city and the problems that kept them apart.

He drove carefully, but as fast as possible, on the rain-slick streets. The absence of other vehicles on the street went unnoticed until headlights suddenly came up behind them. He slowed slightly thinking it might be the police. His bootlegging occupation made him leery of all types of law enforcement. He watched for the lights to pull out to pass them, but they only grew closer.

Edward heard a loud pop and the back window of the truck shattered. Rachel lurched forward and screamed, clutching her left shoulder.

"Oh, God, Edward!" she groaned. "What's happening?"

Edward knew what was happening. Lewis had told him another bootlegging operation wanted his territory. Whoever was following them must think Lewis was driving the truck, returning from a delivery, and they wanted him dead.

"Get down, Rachel, and hang on." Edward floored the accelerator.

Bullets continued to pepper the back of the truck as the two vehicles careened through the city. Streetlights illuminated the unfolding drama. When they reached the outskirts and left the streetlights behind, the shiny black ribbon of road could be seen only as far as the headlights reached. The bullets stopped and Edward looked in the rearview mirror, hoping he had lost the pursuing car, but the lights behind him appeared closer. He tried to get more speed out of the old truck. The sharp curve was suddenly there before him with no warning. Edward hit the brakes. Wet pavement gave no traction to the tires. There was no slowing as the truck hurled sideways over the embankment at the side of the road and rolled.

The car behind slowed and came to a stop on the curve. Three men got out. One, in a fine suit, waited by the car. The other two slid and climbed down to the overturned truck. After a few minutes, they climbed back up to the car and tried to clean some of the mud from their clothes and shoes in front of their headlights.

One of the men stopped cleaning mud, and looked back down into the ditch. "Shit! It was just the kid and some girl. They're both dead. Damn, that makes me feel bad. I just wanted to get Lewis."

The man in the fine suit shrugged. "Oh, well. We'll get him next time."

All three got back in the car and drove away.

Aspen and Willow hovered by their charges, waiting for them to awaken.

"At least they're together this time," Willow said.

Edward and Rachel slowly opened their eyes and reached for each other.

The guardians let them embrace briefly before Aspen spoke softly. "Rachel, I'm here. So is Willow. Do you know what happened?"

The couple drew apart and looked at each other, then at Aspen and Willow.

"Not exactly," Rachel said. She shook her head trying to clear the confusion. "I guess we messed up on trying to run away. Or maybe we didn't. We're together and that's what matters."

Edward smiled sadly. "Didn't I tell you I'd take you somewhere your father couldn't find you?"

Rachel looked at Aspen. "Will mother be all right now? And Hildi and Lewis?

Aspen spread his hands on each side of Rachel, and his glow encircled her. "It's time to leave the problems of this world behind and return home. Think no more about it."

Willow's glow encircled Edward and they all departed.

Chapter 5

Aspen and Willow waited patiently by the steps. The massive building towered above them, the top obscured in clouds. The sides swept away in both directions. The beauty of the architecture was beyond description. This was the home of Them and many, many others that dealt with the education system those on Earth called life.

Edward and Rachel had not waited to be called this time. They had requested the meeting after many days of talking, meditation and prayer. Aspen and Willow knew the reason for the requested meeting. Edward and Rachel wanted to grow old together on Earth. They were asking for special intervention to make that possible. The reasoning they would present to Them for making this request was that they could learn so much more if they were together for a longer time. Very few had ever asked for this so directly. Neither Aspen nor Willow knew what the outcome of the meeting would be.

A messenger hurried down the steps and stopped before the guardians. He held two slips of paper.

"Edward and Rachel have just left. Here are your destinations. Everyone is very excited about this. We all wish you a joyous journey." He handed the papers to Willow and Aspen and ran back up the steps, disappearing through the large open portal.

Willow and Aspen looked at their paper, exchanged broad smiles and departed.

1940
Dallas

Sibyl smiled at the doctor as he walked into the room. She raised herself up from the bed with her elbows. The large white room contained several beds, most occupied by women in different stages of birth labor.

"Surprised to see me, Dr. Martin?" She laughed. "That tumor you said I had is ready to be born."

Dr. Martin stopped by the bed and smiled ruefully.

"Why didn't you come back to see me? You walked out of my office seven months ago and the next time I hear from you, you're here."

"I knew it wasn't a tumor and I wasn't about to let you start cutting on me. I've waited too long for this. I know you think I'm too old to be having a baby but I guess God doesn't think that." She gasped and settled back on the bed as another contraction came.

"No, I don't think you're too old. I did think you couldn't have a child, but you have definitely proven me wrong. Now let's see how long this unexpected miracle plans to wait before making an appearance." Dr. Martin began the examination.

Aspen was happy. The older couple obviously loved each other dearly. They were tolerant, understanding and they shared a strong faith. Rachel had picked wisely. This would be a home of love and caring.

Outside Toledo

A cold blast of air and a few snowflakes preceded the young man through the door. He yanked the cap from his head and hung it on a hook on the backside of the door. His heavy coat followed. The covering of snow on both immediately began to melt and drip on the floor in the warmth of the room.

"It's no use, Honey. Even if I could get the car out of the garage, the roads are closed. It's a good foot deep now and coming down hard."

Honey looked at her husband from her place on the couch and took a deep breath.

"Well, Bobby. It looks like you're going to have to do it."

"Oh, no." He picked up the small child that stood by Honey. "I wasn't even around when this one was born. I was at work. Remember? I don't know what to do. Maybe I can get help over at the Ferguson place." He put the child down and reached for his coat and hat.

"Sorry, Bobby. It isn't going to wait that long. I'll tell you what to do. You just have to do it." Honey laughed. "And besides, I'll be doing most of the work."

Her laughter was short lived as a hard contraction made her clutch the arm of the couch.

"God help us." Bobby paled. "Okay. I'll put Petey in his room and get him interested in his toys and then you tell me what to do." Bobby started from the room with Petey, but paused at the door. "I love you, Honey."

"I love you too."

Willow heard the exchange with pleasure. Edward would soon start his life in this beautiful countryside, even though its beauty right now was making things a little difficult for Edward's parents.

He visited briefly with Petey's guardian who was keeping the young boy occupied. Petey was still young enough to see his guardian and didn't mind spending some time in his room playing with his constant companion. This was a good home, a good starting place for Edward's life this time.

1950

Rachel liked the feel of the thick grass under her back. She looked up at the night sky and marveled at all the beautiful, tiny lights that looked back at her.

Sibyl stood just inside the kitchen door smiling out at Rachel.

"Rachel, it's getting late. You better come in now and get to bed. We have a big day ahead of us tomorrow unpacking everything."

Rachel sat up slowly and turned slightly to see her mother.

"Mama, is this place really ours? Nobody can come and tell us to move or anything?"

"Yes, it's really ours. We'll be here a long time and you'll have lots of chances to look at the sky."

"There's a lot more stars here than in Dallas. Why is that, Mama, when we only moved a few miles?"

Sibyl laughed at Rachel's perplexed expression. She stepped out on the porch and looked up at the splendor that had captivated Rachel.

"There are no street lights here, or lighted signs. And there's no next-door neighbor with a porch light on. We're in the country now." Sibyl swatted at a mosquito that landed on her arm. "We've got lots of country bugs now too so you better come on in before you get eat up."

"Okay, mama, but just a little while longer. Please?"

"A few more minutes then. When I get out of the shower you have to come in." She walked back into the house.

Rachel resumed her position on the grass and smiled. The small, two bedroom, one bath frame house was much nicer than any she had ever lived in. The acre of land surrounding it had grass and trees and a nice place for the garden her mother had always wanted. She felt safe and happy.

The longer she looked up at the stars, the more it seemed they were trying to tell her something but she couldn't quite make out what it was. She sensed that it was something very important and grand.

Ohio

"Come on Edward. There's going to be a full moon tonight, and the dogs are having a fit to go. They know when it's a good coon hunting night." Petey checked his gun carefully as he talked.

Edward sat on the porch steps looking up at the star-studded sky.

"I heard you tell dad you were going to kill that coon, not just tree it. You know I don't like to kill nothing. Why do you want to kill that poor old coon anyway? He never did nothing to you." Edward turned his eyes from the sky and studied his brother standing beside him on the porch.

"Something keeps getting in the chicken house and eating eggs. That's doing something to me." Petey stepped off the porch. The dogs milled around his legs, eager to go.

"That's probably a skunk. And we still get plenty of eggs. You never missed a breakfast." Edward looked his brother up and down and smiled. "Or any other meal from the looks of you."

"I'm just hefty. That's what Dad says. Besides, I'd rather be like me than a skinny sissy like you." Petey turned and started across the yard, the three happy coon dogs at his heels.

"Just be careful. I won't be there to get you out of trouble." Edward grinned.

Petey raised his hand in a wave without turning.

1954
Texas

"Come on Rachel. It'll be fun. Mike's big brother got us a six pack." The voice on the phone was insistent.

"No, Bonnie. I've got to finish this history report. I got an eighty on that test last week and I've got to bring that up."

"So what. I flunked that test but it's not going to keep me from having fun. Don't be a square. It's still warm enough to swim at the lake and all the good looking guys are going to be there."

"Well, have fun and I'll see you Monday at school. Bye." Rachel hung up the phone but stood with her hand on the receiver, suddenly unsure of her decision.

"You did the right thing, Rachel." Aspen hovered close beside her. "You're still a child. Don't try to grow up too fast. Remember you have plenty of time and Edward is in your future."

Rachel smiled and took her hand from the phone. A feeling of happiness softly settled over her. She left the phone on the small shelf in the hall and returned to her room where the books and papers waited for her, scattered across the bed.

Ohio

Edward didn't like Mondays. He didn't like the larger school he attended now. He hadn't minded when his parents moved the family into town. The new friends were fun. He and Petey had played and hung out together at their country home, but the older they got, the less they had in common.

He walked along the now familiar street, not even having to think about the direction his feet took him. School would be at the end of his walk, but the warm September day beckoned his feet to take another direction.

Dick and Mitch were skipping today and going fishing. They had told him yesterday afternoon after the neighborhood baseball game. The creek would be perfect today. The feel of summer lingered in the air and the trees were still green.

Edward stopped at a cross street. A right turn would take him to school. To the left a few blocks was the bridge and the creek where he knew Dick and Mitch would be waiting. He grinned, turned to the left and walked faster.

Willow flapped his wings furiously as he faced Edward and tried to stop the fast pace in the wrong direction.

"No, Edward. You need to go to school. You'll get in trouble if you don't go. It will disappoint your parents." Willow could feel the shield Edward had put up to block his advice. He did that often now.

With a resigned sigh, Willow let Edward pass him and resumed his place at Edward's back. When they reached the creek and joined Dick and Mitch, one of the other guardians looked at Willow with a wry smile and shrugged his shoulders. The movement was emphasized by his wings. The euphoric mood of the boys was contagious and the guardians found themselves enjoying the stolen and forbidden day. It would be the first of many that year.

1956
Texas

"Rachel, you're sixteen now and your father and I have decided you can start dating. Mrs. Gaines and I have been talking. You know her son, Tom. He's a grade ahead of you and a very nice boy. Well, we feel you two should get to know each other and if you'd like to go to a movie together, that would be fine with us."

Sibyl smiled nervously as she continued to wipe the already clean kitchen counter top. The rehearsed words came out clipped and unnatural sounding. She and Rachel's father had talked about this time and now she wished it wasn't here. The years had gone by too fast.

Rachel's childhood had been such a joy to the older couple. When she first started to school, they joined the younger parents in all the activities with enthusiasm. Rachel always did well in school and never gave them any problems. She did seem quieter and a little more studious than the other children. For this they were grateful, but as she grew older, they became concerned. She was happy to remain at home and read while her friends went to lake parties, roller skating and badgered their parents to let them start driving the family car.

Sibyl finally confided her concerns to a fellow PTA member, Mrs. Gaines, and was delighted to learn they shared that concern. Tom also stayed at home and was an avid reader. His only outside activities was the junior aeronautics meetings and a chess club. The two decided their children were perfect for each other and should start dating.

Sibyl had to give her rehearsed speech today. If Mrs. Gaines' part of the plan worked, Tom would be calling Rachel this afternoon for a movie date.

"I don't know, Mom. I barely know Tom, just to say hi in the hall sometimes. He's really smart but he wears funny looking clothes and a lot of the kids tease him and call him egg head, four eyes, and stuff like that. Besides, why would he ask me for a date? Did you and his mom come up with this idea?" Rachel looked at her mother, but Sibyl wouldn't meet her eyes.

"Not exactly." Sibyl suddenly decided the top of the refrigerator needed cleaning and pulled a kitchen chair in front of it to stand in. "The Gaines are nice people and sometimes we talk at the PTA meetings. I may have mentioned that we thought you were old enough to start dating."

Rachel started to leave the room but turned back and saw her mother's flushed face and guilty expression.

"You did! You asked Mrs. Gaines to fix me up with her son. I'm humiliated! When he calls, I'll just tell him no." Rachel ran from the kitchen.

Sibyl climbed down from the chair, scooted it back to the table and sat down. She knew she hadn't handled that well. It had been so much easier to be a parent when Rachel was younger. With a resigned sigh, she got up, pushed the chair back to the refrigerator and climbed on it. At least the refrigerator would have a clean top.

A few hours later the phone rang. Sibyl and Jake were sitting outside so Rachel had to answer it.

"Is this Rachel?"

"Yes."

"This is Tom ... Tom Gaines. I was wondering ... uh ... if you didn't have any plans tonight ... uh..."

Rachel heard the nervous uncertainty in his voice and felt as sorry for him as she had felt for herself earlier today.

"I don't have any plans, Tom."

"There's a good movie on at the Carrollton theater. Would you like to go?"

"Sure. What time?"

"It starts at seven. I could pick you up about six thirty. I know that doesn't give you much time to get ready but ..."

"I'll be ready," Rachel interrupted. "See you then." She hung the phone up and giggled. His call had sounded so pitiful, she just couldn't tell him no. Now she knew someone else felt as nervous and scared about this dating thing as she did.

Ohio

The three boys waited nervously in the alley behind the store. They trusted Charlie but something could happen and if the wrong thing happened, Charlie and all of them would be in big trouble.

It seemed to them that Charlie had been gone a long time. The itch to run was building to a high level.

Charlie turned the corner of the building and the boys let out a sigh. He carried a paper bag. His grin told them everything was fine.

Edward reached for the bag. "Was there any change?" he asked as he held the bag against him and felt the cold contents through the paper.

Charlie's grin broadened and he put his hand in his pocket, jingling the loose coins.

"A little but that's what you call carrying charges. I carried it from the store to you. Now go drink your beer and if you get caught, I don't know you." Charlie turned and walked from the alley.

Dick pried the sack from Edward's chest far enough to look into it.

"He got it. A quart for each. Let's go."

They hurried down the alley, Edward holding the sack tightly against him to prevent the bottles from rattling.

Willow circled Edward and projected his words as forcefully as possible.

"Edward, stop! You know this is wrong. You're not old enough to drink. Remember the last time you did this? How sick you got? Your parents will find out again. You love your parents. You don't want to hurt them. Edward, listen to me! STOP!"

Edward stopped. Mitch and Dick went several paces past him before they also stopped and looked back at Edward. Their guardians were also clamoring. If the living world could have heard the ruckus the guardians were making, many would be running from their houses to see what was wrong. But the living world could not hear them. Their own charges couldn't hear them unless they listened carefully and quietly. The three boys did not want to listen carefully and to listen quietly was out of the question.

"Why are you stopping, Edward? Let's go." Mitch took a step back toward Edward. "I like my beer cold so let's get to the woods before it gets hot."

The boys resumed the fast pace and soon disappeared into the deep shade of the woods.

1958
Texas

Rachel peered into the mirror and frowned at the reflection she saw.

"I won't go." Her voice sounded close to tears. "Not with this horrible thing on my face. It looks like a third eye. Why did this have to happen now?" She threw herself face down on the bed.

Sibyl sat down by her and stroked the back of her head. The long black hair felt satin smooth under her hand.

"It's only a pimple, Rachel. Everyone gets them sometime. We'll comb your bangs a little lower on your forehead and no one will even notice. Besides, Tom won't care. He's seen you with pimples before. That boy really cares a lot for you and he came home from college just to take you to the senior prom. Now don't cry or your eyes will get all red and puffy."

Rachel turned over onto her back and stared forlornly at the ceiling.

"That's another problem, Mama. Tom does care about me. I guess I should have told you. In the last letter I got from him before he came home this time, he asked me to marry him in three years, after he graduates. I like Tom a lot and we've had fun together but I don't love him that way. I don't want to hurt him but I'm not about to marry him. He's my best friend. Just a best friend."

Tears slipped from the corners of Rachel's eyes and trickled unhindered into the edge of her hair.

Sibyl was stunned but tried not to show it. She and Jake had come to assume Rachel would marry Tom. Rachel's talk of college had been met with condescending smiles and more or less ignored. Rachel might attend some college but would marry Tom before she finished. They would live close by and have children which the grandparents would take turns baby sitting and spoiling.

"Rachel, you don't really mean that. Tom's crazy about you and will take good care of you, and the children you will have. You're just upset now because of that silly pimple. Please don't tell Tom all this until you've had time to think about it. The best marriages start out as friendships. You just get up and go take a long bubble bath. Tom will be right on time, like he always is, to pick you up for the prom. Dependability is a very good trait in a young man."

Sibyl stood up and smoothed an imaginary wrinkle from the perfectly pressed formal hanging on the closet door. She didn't want to think about Rachel's words and how it might change the plans she had for her daughter's future.

Ohio

Edward sat on the edge of his chair at the kitchen table and fidgeted. Honey sat across from him and Bobby at the end. Honey held the paper of doom and studied it carefully. Everything was too quiet.

She handed the paper to Bobby and fixed her gaze on Edward. Edward quickly looked down at his hands that rested on the yellow Formica tabletop. He started to get up from the chair.

"I need to go to the bathroom."

"Sit!"

His mother didn't raise her voice but the single word put him hurriedly back in the chair.

Bobby cleared his throat and put the papers down in front of him.

"How many times have we talked about you skipping school?" Bobby didn't wait for an answer. "Did you ever think about what it would do to your grades? Did you think we wouldn't find out?"

"No, sir. I just thought ... "

"No, you didn't think," Bobby interrupted. "Now you aren't going to graduate. You aren't going to get that job Mr. Barns was holding for you. You've put Petey in a really bad position. He went out on a limb convincing Mr. Barns to hold that job open for you, telling him what a good worker you are. I guess he'll see now that you aren't. You wouldn't even work hard enough to pass your senior year."

Bobby shoved the papers across the table and got up.

"Well, that's it. You can go back to school next year or get a job, if you can find one. I'm through worrying with it. One thing for certain," Bobby put his hands on the table and leaned toward Edward. "I won't give you another cent. If you want your cigarettes and beer and running around money, you can earn it yourself." With those words he straightened and walked from the room. A few seconds later the front door slammed.

Edward sat dejected and silent looking at the scattered papers. The sarcastic sound of his father's last words hurt worse than a physical blow.

Honey finally broke the silence.

"Well, Edward. I guess it's up to you now. Sounds like your play days are over. Do you have any ideas about what you're going to do to straighten up this mess you've gotten yourself into?"

Edward kept his gaze lowered for a few minutes. He didn't want to see the disappointment he knew was in his mother's eyes. With a resigned sigh, he sat back in his chair and looked up. The face across from him reflected the look he expected.

"Guess I better get busy and find a job. I'll try to get one so I can work evenings when school starts."

He saw tears forming in Honey's eyes and felt the answering tightness in his own throat.

"No time like the present to start." He pushed his chair back and almost ran from the room. The reality of adulthood had hit him hard and he didn't want his mother to see the tears he knew would come. Already the childish actions of the past were whirling in his mind.

Willow followed closely behind.

"Edward, I truly wish you could have seen the wrongness of those things when you were doing them. But now you do. Everything will work out if you keep the same thoughts you have now. I'll try to be more helpful but you've got to start listening to me better." Willow felt the walls in Edward's mind crumbling as he talked. Now he would be heard.

1959
Texas

Rachel sat in a big leather chair facing the man behind the desk. She heard the words he said but the meaning was lost to her. He was Mr. Gorman, an attorney, one of her father's fishing buddies.

Her parents had never had much money but Jake's reputation as a fishing expert had drawn an eclectic group of men to him. It was only a hobby but Jake always seemed to know where the best fish were biting. Now that hobby had taken both her parents from her.

A boating accident. A sudden storm. It wasn't supposed to storm in Texas in August.

Rachel's mind was locked into that day in early August when a sheriff's car had pulled into the drive and two men in uniform came to the door. Three weeks had now passed and Rachel still waited for the nightmare to be over. She knew she would soon wake up and go to her part-time job at Moore's Bar-B-Que. Sibyl would be taking her shopping for clothes to start her next year at North Texas University.

"Rachel, I think this is a more than fair offer for the house. They're taking into consideration the value of the land around you that has been re-zoned commercial even though your place hasn't. Between that and the insurance, it will be enough to see you through three more years of college with plenty left over to get you started in whatever field of work you want. About the cars, I'd advise you to sell yours and keep your parents. It's a lot newer and in much better shape. The probate on the will should be finished in a few weeks and all this can be finalized. If you need any money before then, I'll be glad to loan it to you. Do you have any questions?"

Rachel stared dumbly across the desk for several minutes.

"Rachel?"

"Oh, yeah, questions. Money." Her speech was as disjointed as her thoughts.

"No, I don't need anything. I went back to work this week and that will pay for food and gas."

Mr. Gorman could see Rachel still wasn't fully aware of the situation she was in.

"What about utility bills? And books for this next semester? My son has already bought his and I know they aren't cheap."

Seeing the uncomprehending look on Rachel's face, Mr. Gorman scooted in his chair so he could reach his wallet in his back pocket. He did some quick mental computation, counted out a sum of money and pushed it across the desk to Rachel.

"When the utility bills come in, go pay them in cash and get a receipt. You're already enrolled for this semester so go to the bookstore by the campus and get the ones you need. My son got used ones and they were a lot less expensive but you get what you want. I'll call you if you need to sign any papers before the probate is finished." Mr. Gorman spoke as he got up and walked around the desk. He picked up the money Rachel hadn't touched and put it in her hands.

"You call me if you need anything or if any problems come up." He helped her from the chair and guided her to the door. He watched her walk across the reception area and out the door, still holding the money in her closed fist. He shook his head sadly, stepped through the door, and turned to his receptionist.

"If Rachel calls, put her straight through, no matter what I'm doing or who I'm with."

She nodded in understanding.

Ohio

Supper was on the table and it was a big one, unusual for a Saturday night. Petey had come to eat with them and Honey moved the Sunday dinner meal up to tonight.

Edward reached for a chicken leg, roasted to a golden brown. His hands appeared dirty even though he had scrubbed them with Lava soap and a brush. The job at the service station left its mark on him. That had been his place of employment through his senior year and continued now with more hours.

The congenial conversation at the table was interrupted by the ringing phone. Honey went to the hall to answer it and returned in a minute.

"It's for you, Edward. Dick's calling from Texas."

The scowl on her face let Edward know she still remembered the escapades he, Dick and Mitch pulled when they were in school together. Dick had managed somehow to graduate the year the other two boys failed and left town shortly afterwards. His intermittent letters came from Texas.

"Hi, Dick. What's going on?" Edward grinned broadly into the phone. It was the first time Dick had called since he had been gone.

"Hey, Edward. Keeping out of trouble?"

"It's no fun getting into trouble without you here. Besides, you were the one who always thought up the things we got in trouble for." Edward laughed.

"You still working at the station?" Dick asked.

"Yeah, it has benefits so I still hang out there."

"What kind of benefits can you have at that place?"

Edward extended his hand in front of him as if Dick could see it over the phone.

"Girls get a look at my hands and know I'm a mechanic. You'd be surprised at how many girls I've ended up dating because they need work done on their cars. That's a big benefit."

Edward didn't want Dick to know his real feelings about his job. He knew his parents had wanted more for him and he wanted more.

His small salary made it necessary to live at his parent's home. Petey had moved out on his own a few months after he graduated and had bought a good used car. Edward still walked to work and borrowed the family car if he went out at night, which he seldom did. The job possibilities in this town decreased steadily as all the big plants moved south, one after the other. Petey had been lucky to get the job he had and Edward knew he had thrown away the chance for a similar position.

"Well, if you can tear yourself away from all those benefits, there's a good job here with your name on it."

Edward glanced around the corner to see if his parents were paying any attention to his phone call. His mother was looking at him. He picked the phone up from the hall table, edged around the corner into his bedroom, and softly pushed the door partially closed.

"What kind of job?"

"There's an opening where I work, on the college campus. It's in the maintenance department. I've got a swell boss. He promised to hold it open 'til I could talk to you. You can room with me. I've got a two-bedroom apartment and the roomy I got now doesn't pay his share half the time. I was ready to throw him out before this job thing came up. What do you think?" There was a hopeful tone to Dick's question.

Edward's mind spun with thoughts. Leave this town with it's dead-end job possibilities, out on his own for the first time, see Dick again and have fun with his old friend. A slight qualm briefly flitted through his mind ... leaving his parents to go so far away.

"What kind of salary do they pay?"

The amount Dick gave was almost twice what he made at the station.

"Dick, give me your number and let me call you back in a little while. I need to finish eating supper. Then I'll digest mom's chicken and the job offer at the same time." Edward grabbed a pencil and an envelope off his dresser and wrote the number.

"Okay. Got it. Don't go anywhere. I'll be calling in an hour or so."

Edward went back to the table to finish eating. He didn't hear much of the conversation for the rest of the meal.

Willow's soft but insistent words filled Edwards mind. To Edward, they seemed like his own thoughts.

"It's time to go, to move on. You're a grown man now. You want to make your parents proud of you. This is your chance to turn around all the failures of the past. You need to go to Texas. Rachel is waiting."

The last thought didn't come clear to Edward. Anticipation of something unknown curled through his body. Sudden resolve filled him.

"I'm going to Texas."

The statement came in the middle of Petey's story of an incident at his job. In shocked surprise, three pairs of eyes turned to him at the now silent table.

"Dick's found a good job for me at the college where he works. He said I could share his apartment. I'll make a lot more money than at any job I could get in this town. I guess I'll be leaving next weekend, Friday night or Saturday morning. Got to check the bus schedules and give my boss notice."

The announcement made, Edward turned his attention back to his plate and the unfinished meal.

Honey was the first to find her voice.

"Are you out of your mind? I know Dick, and if the two of you get together you'll be in some kind of trouble in less than a week. We *won't* send money to Texas to get you out of jail. I can't believe you'd . . ."

Bobby interrupted her with a raised hand.

"Now wait a minute. We haven't seen Dick in a year. Maybe he's grown up like Edward here. We can't go blaming those other boys for all the trouble Edward got into. I'm sure he had a lot to do with it. This last year he's shown us what a decent young man he is. He worked hard and finished school too. If he thinks this is a good chance for him, he has my blessings."

Very early the next Saturday morning the whole family saw Edward off at the bus station with all their blessings.

Texas

Edward and Dick sat on the small patio of their apartment. Edward read his letter from home while Dick watched the burgers cooking on the grill. Neither man was much of a cook but they could prepare eatable meat over charcoal. They both preferred it well done.

"Mom says they already have snow. She wouldn't believe me if I told her we are sitting out here in short sleeves."

Edward continued reading while Dick got up to check the burgers. A look of concern formed on his face as he turned the page over to read the last part on the back.

Dick turned from the grill and saw Edward's expression.

"Problems at home?"

"It's my Uncle Arthur. You know, Dad's oldest brother. He's in the hospital and they don't expect him to live." Edward dropped the letter on the small table beside him and gazed across the low brick wall that surrounded the patio.

"Damn! He's my favorite uncle. Remember when you used to come over to the house when he was there? He'd sit on the front porch and play his guitar for us. It was just old country stuff but he was so good, we listened anyway."

"I'm really sorry to hear that. Yeah, I remember. Your mom would bring out glasses of lemonade and we'd sit there and listen and watch the lightning bugs come out."

Both young men sat in silence, their minds reaching back to the time of childhood when their lives were much simpler.

When the meat was done, they carried it inside and finished the evening in a somber mood.

The first ring of the phone jarred Edward awake. He'd been expecting the call ever since he received the letter. Any time the phone rings in the middle of the night, it usually means something bad.

"Hello." Edward heard his mother's voice and the message he knew was coming. "That's Okay, Mom. I wanted you to call. You know how I felt about Uncle Arthur. I'll be on the next bus."

He hung the phone up and turned to see Dick coming from his own bedroom.

"Sorry that woke you up too."

"That's Okay. It's your uncle?"

"Yeah." Edward sat on the couch, put his face in his hands and fought the tears that burned his eyes.

"Can I do anything?" Dick sat beside his friend and put his arm across his shoulders.

"I need to catch the next bus out that's headed in that direction. Can you call the bus station for me and find that out? I'll go pack a few things."

"Sure, go ahead. I'll take care of it."

Edward rubbed his face roughly, wiping the tears away in the process. He gave himself a shake and got up from the couch. At his bedroom door he thought of something else and turned.

"Can you tell the boss about this and tell him I'll be back as soon as I can. I don't want to loose my job."

"I'll tell him first thing in the morning. Don't worry about it. He'll understand. Besides, you have some sick days accumulated already. They can just take your time off that."

Edward went in his room and packed.

Edward sat with his head against the back of the bus seat. His jacket was balled up to create a pillow of sorts between the side of his head and the window. The last five days had been exhausting but he was still unable to sleep.

There had been little rest at his parent's home. Several out of town relatives had stayed there and he felt compelled to let them use his old bedroom while he tried to sleep on the couch in the living room.

Everyone stayed up late talking. His mother would be in the kitchen at first light preparing breakfast for everyone. The emotional strain was much harder than he had expected. Often his father would break into tears.

Sometime during those days the thought came to him that he or Petey would be experiencing this same thing some day. After that, he sought out Petey at every opportunity and talked to him. They got to know each other better than they had in years. When the family took him to the bus, both brothers cried and embraced each other.

Edward might have rested a little easier had it not been for the thing he held in his lap ... Uncle Arthur's guitar in the battered old case. He refused to let it be put with the other luggage in the compartments below. The overhead rack was crowded and he wouldn't chance having it pulled out by accident. The seat next to him was vacant but if he put it there, someone might take it if he went to sleep. So he held it as he would hold a child with the neck extending up over his left shoulder.

He was surprised when his aunt placed it in his hands. Uncle Arthur had remembered the front porch evenings too, and left instructions Edward was to have his guitar. Now it was Edward's treasure to be protected and cherished.

Rachel hurried down the hall, anxious to get home. Home was a small apartment over the garage of a private home. Mr. Gorman had helped her relocate close to the campus with Mr. and Mrs. Shaffer who were friends of his. The quiet, peaceful place was much better than the dorm room she had first considered. The Shaffers welcomed her with compassion and understanding.

As she maneuvered through a group of other students, she momentarily had resentful thoughts about Toby. Toby was a friend and had two classes with her. Now she carried his guitar as she always did three days a week. He had one class after his music class and had asked

Rachel at the first of spring semester if she would mind carrying his guitar home. He would pick it up on the way to his apartment, just a block from her. At that time it seemed logical and, Rachel had thought, no problem. Usually she didn't mind, but today she looked for anything to be angry about.

The letter from Tom seemed to add extra weight to her book satchel. She had picked up yesterday's mail this morning and read it in the parking lot before she went into her first class.

Tom had written "I've decided the wedding date should be moved up to this summer. Although I'll still have another year before I get my degree, I know I can take care of you. Having discussed this with my parents, they are willing to help financially during that time."

Rachel was furious. She mumbled to herself as she tried to open the heavy door at the end of the hall. Half the mumbling was about the guitar that hampered her and half was at Tom.

"Why did I ever agree to carry this thing? Where does he get off telling me I'm going to marry him? I never said I would. Take care of me? Bull sh –"

Her outburst was brought to a sudden halt as the door swung open and she fell forward into the base of a ladder. The ladder swayed dangerously before the young man standing at the side caught and righted it.

"Whoa, Sweety. Hope you don't drive like you walk."

Edward held the bottom of the latter as Dick, standing at the top, steadied himself against the near wall. They were replacing burned out light bulbs in the entranceway.

Rachel bent to retrieve her purse she had dropped in the collision.

"It's none of your business how I drive."

Edward had released his hold on the ladder and bent for the purse also. Their heads cracked together.

They were suddenly face-to-face, bent over, both holding a side of the purse. Edward grinned broadly. Rachel frowned in aggravation. Their expressions changed as they slowly stood up, each still holding the purse.

Several seconds passed in silence. Dick finally broke the quiet.

"Edward, are you going to hand me that new light bulb or stand there flirting? Get her phone number so you can get back to work."

When that remark got no response, Dick climbed down the ladder and picked up the bulb from the box close by. Another group of students came out and parted around the couple. Dick took a step and stood by them.

"This is Edward. I'm Dick. Tell him your name and what ever information is necessary so we can finish our job before quitting time."

"Rachel ... I'm Rachel. Sorry about running into your ladder." Her eyes never left Edward's face and she wanted to reach up and rub a small smudge of dirt off his cheek.

Edward loosened his hold on her purse.

"You go to school here?" Edward asked and groaned inwardly. That was a stupid question, he thought.

"Yes ... yes I do." Rachel didn't see anything wrong with the question.

"You play the guitar?" Edward motioned to the case she carried.

"No, it belongs to a friend. He's still in class so I'm taking it home. He's just a friend. I'm just ..." Rachel stopped when she realized she was babbling.

"I've got a guitar. I don't know how to play it yet, but I'm going to learn." In a sudden burst of sanity, Edward asked, "Can I have your phone number and call you sometime. Maybe we could go out to dinner and I can show you my guitar."

Rachel had never given her phone number to a stranger but, as her emotions continued their crazy upward spiral, she found the numbers tumbling from her lips as Edward wrote them rapidly on a scrap of paper he had produced from his pocket, along with a stub of a pencil. Without any words of parting, she backed slowly away from him, turned and ran to her car.

Willow and Aspen hovered close. Their glow of happiness obvious to anyone that cared to notice, but none did.

Aspen studied the two human faces closely.

"Do you think they may be remembering?" he asked Willow.

"They aren't supposed to. If everyone did their jobs properly, there would be no past memory. Of course, things did happen pretty fast and this was a special case. Who knows?"

Aspen folded his arms, floated back a few paces and looked at the couple with sublime bliss.

"I'm not going to question it. I'm just relieved the blessed meeting has

happened. I know there have been many guardians working toward this time. Now we only need pray for a smooth continuation for them."

The guardians parted as did their charges, knowing they would meet again soon and anticipated that meeting with much joy.

"Listen, Tom. Just shut up a minute and listen. I did not say I would marry you." Rachel paced the floor as far as the phone cord would reach. "I told you I would think about it. That's all. Just think about it. We've been friends a long time, and I don't want that to change. But if you insist on our relationship going further, then it will change. I love you as a friend. Not the marrying kind of love."

Rachel stopped pacing and listened. Tears came to her eyes, and she slowly sat down in the chair next to the phone.

"I'm sorry you feel that way. Call me if you change your mind." She hung the phone up and stared at it for a moment. A sob shook her body. She buried her face in her hands as tears tore from her.

The ache in her heart jumbled with her thoughts. Losing Tom hurts. He stood by me after my parents' death, always being there when I needed him. Am I making a mistake? Should I marry him, and try to learn to love him as a wife? I still need his friendship. What will life be like if Tom isn't there to talk to, to write long letters to? He understands me better than anyone.

She reached for the phone, but stopped herself. No. He needs time to think about this. I know our friendship is important to him, too. I'll call him tomorrow. He didn't mean the things he said.

The sobs subsided, and the tears slowed. Rachel sniffed and looked around for a tissue but saw only an empty box. She got up and went to the bathroom. In the middle of a noisy nose blowing, she heard a knock on her door. She looked at her watch.

"Just a minute, Toby." She quickly wet a washcloth and bathed her face. A glance in the mirror made her grimace. Her eyes were red and puffy.

On the way to the door, she picked up the guitar case. Toby was smiling, as usual, when she opened the door. His smile changed to a look of concern when he saw Rachel.

"What's wrong, kid? You look like you just lost your best friend."

"Oh, Toby." The tears started again. Rachel shoved the guitar at him and ran back to the bathroom.

Toby sat the guitar on the floor and followed Rachel.

"Rachel, I'm sorry. What happened? Come on out of there and talk to me." Toby talked to the closed bathroom door.

"I'm okay. Just go away." The words were muffled.

"No, I'm not going to go away until I know what's wrong with you." Toby waited a moment. When only silence answered him, he tapped insistently on the door. "I'm not leaving. You may as well come on out. I'll stay here all night if I have to."

He finally heard Rachel blowing her nose.

"Okay. Give me a minute."

Toby found himself a seat on the small couch and waited. Rachel came out of the bathroom carrying a roll of toilet paper.

"I'm out of tissues." Rachel sat in the chair facing Toby.

"So I see." Toby tried to stay serious, but the sight of Rachel sitting there, clutching a roll of toilet paper, was too much. His suppressed grin turned into a chuckle.

The corners of Rachel's mouth twitched up. She looked down at the toilet paper and then up at Toby. They both burst into laughter.

"I'm sorry," Toby was finally able to say. "I'm not being very sympathetic to whatever is bothering you, am I?"

Rachel rolled off a length of paper and wiped her eyes that were now filled with laughter tears.

"That's okay." Rachel blew her nose again. That set both of them off laughing again.

"It's Tom." Rachel became serious. "I'm having a problem with him."

"Is that the brainy stuffed shirt I met at the football game?"

"Yes, that's Tom. I got a letter from him, and..."

"Wait a minute. This sounds like it may be a long story, and I'm starving. Let's walk over to the burger joint and you can tell me all about it while we eat."

"Right now? I look a mess."

"You look fine. Just a little red eyed. Go work some of that women's magic with makeup. I really am starving so hurry. Didn't eat lunch today."

"Okay, but if anyone says anything about how I look, I'm going to tell them you beat me."

Rachel got a bottle of cold water from the refrigerator and took it to the bathroom with her. She emerged in a few minutes and looked much better.

The walk in the afternoon warmth of the spring day was refreshing. Rachel was much calmer now, and began explaining her problem to Toby. He was a good listener. The conversation continued as they got their food and chose an outside table on the patio of the café.

"You did the right thing." Toby talked between bites. "You can't marry someone when all you feel is friendship. Sure, friendship is important, but there's got to be passion, desire. You have to feel like you can't live without being with them."

"That's the problem." Rachel pushed her half eaten burger to the center of the table. "You can have the rest of that if you want it."

"Thanks." Toby pushed his empty plate to the side and pulled Rachel's uneaten portion to him.

Rachel leaned back in the chair and took another drink of her soda. "Tom's been my friend since high school. We've always been able to talk about anything and everything. I don't know what I would have done if he hadn't been there when my parents died. I can't imagine not having him around to talk to, to confide in, to ask his advise. You're right about him being brainy. He's one of the smartest people I know."

"Well, I take it back about the brainy part. If he was very smart, he wouldn't be pushing you away. You're about the prettiest, nicest girl on this campus. And I'll be glad to help you get over him. How about a date Saturday night?"

Rachel laughed. "Oh, no, Toby. We're not going to ruin our friendship."

She glanced over at the next table as two young men sat down with food. Her laughter died in her throat and butterflies started fluttering in her stomach when she recognized them.

Dick and Edward began eating. Edward sat with his back to Rachel, and Dick sat across the table, facing Rachel. Dick looked over as he chewed. It was hard to smile with his mouth full, but he managed it with a small wave.

Edward turned to see whom Dick waved to. He looked into Rachel's eyes and couldn't break his gaze. He put his sandwich on the table without looking and missed the plate.

"Hi, Rachel." Edward continued to look into Rachel's eyes.

A soft smile curved Rachel's lips. "Hi."

After a few uncomfortable silent minutes, while Dick and Toby looked at each other and the gazing pair, Dick finally broke the quiet and addressed Toby.

"Hi. I'm Dick and the one acting like he's not all here is Edward. We met Rachel earlier today on campus when she tried to knock me off a ladder."

"Uh ... I'm Toby, a friend of Rachel's."

"Are you the guy that plays guitar?"

"Yeah, that's me."

"Maybe you and I should sit together. At least we'd have someone to talk to. Looks like these two have become completely mute."

Edward and Rachel both blinked, and the expression on their faces looked like they had just awakened.

Rachel sat her drink on the table. "I'm sorry. Toby, this is Dick and Edward. They work at the college."

Toby looked at her with a wry grin. "We've already met."

"Oh, I... I didn't know." Rachel was clearly confused.

Toby laughed. "Why don't you join us. Rachel and Edward are going to get cricks in their necks if we stay like this."

Dick stood up and gathered his plate and drink. "Might as well. Come on Edward. Snap out of it."

Edward put his sandwich back on the plate and followed. He set his plate and soda on the table by Rachel, and slowly sat down.

"I really feel like I've met you someplace before," Edward said to Rachel.

Rachel leaned forward with her arms on the table. "I know. But I can't remember where or when."

"Have you ever been to Ohio?"

"No. I've never been north of the Mason-Dixon line. I was born in Dallas, and I've lived around there all my life. Have you been to Dallas?"

"No. Haven't been there yet. Dick keeps telling me he's going to take me there some Saturday."

Dick and Toby began talking about the college, and finally got around to the subject of Toby's guitar lessons. Edward momentarily came out of his dazed fascination with Rachel to ask Toby about taking lessons.

"Sure. I'll be glad to give you some pointers, basic chords, and things like that. My Saturdays are free this semester. How about a time before lunch." Toby had an immediate liking for these young men. And if Edward was interested in guitars, that was even better.

Dick motioned to Edward's plate. "You aren't eating your food. Thought you said you were hungry."

"I'm not hungry now. You can have it if you want it." Edward turned back to Rachel. "What kind of classes are you taking? You going to be a school teacher or something?"

"Just general education classes now. You know, math, English, science, stuff like that. I don't know what I want to do when I get out. I like kids, but I can't see myself as a teacher."

The evening wore on. The waiter cleared the table, and still the foursome sat. Toby was the first to stand up.

"It's been fun, but I've got homework waiting. It was nice meeting you guys." Toby wrote his address and phone number on a napkin and gave it to Edward. "I'll see you Saturday morning. Just give me a call before you come over." He turned to Rachel. "You ready to leave now?"

"Yes. No." She looked at Edward questioningly.

"Would you like to go for a walk, then I'll see you home?" Edward reached across the table and took her hand. The touch unleashed a tornado of emotions through them both.

"That will be nice."

They stood up, still holding hands, and walked out the side gate of the café patio.

Dick and Toby watched them go and turned to each other with a shrug. They shook hands and went out the same gate. Edward and Rachel were walking slowly away, still holding hands, and still looking at each other.

"See ya'," Toby said to Dick and started back to his apartment.

"Yeah." Dick got in his truck parked by the café, shook his head with a grin, and drove home.

Edward stopped walking and leaned against a large oak tree next to the sidewalk. He still held Rachel's hand.

"I know I'm acting like a durn fool, and I'm not. At least I don't think I am." He took her other hand as she turned to face him. "I can't explain it, but there's crazy things going on inside me every time I see you. I swear this has never happened to me before."

"You don't have to explain it, Edward. It's the same with me. I feel like I should know everything about you, like we've been together all our lives or something. And that's weird because I don't know anything about you. My mind keeps going in circles, looking for the memories that should be there, but they're not. It's like I've just forgotten something, and if I think hard enough, I'll remember it."

Edward sighed, dropped Rachel's hands and pulled her against him. He held her close with his face in her hair. Rachel put her arms around him as far as she could. She couldn't reach all the way around because of the tree at his back.

Standing there with her face nestled against his neck felt so natural. He smelled clean and fresh, and familiar.

After a few minutes, Rachel stepped back out of his arms. "Okay. We don't know each other. So let's change that. Tell me about yourself. Where were you born? Where did you grow up? Tell me about your family."

They turned back on the sidewalk, and started walking, hand in hand.

"Well, I was born on a farm outside Toledo, Ohio, in 1940."

They stopped at the bottom of the stairs. Rachel looked at her watch. "It's midnight. We must have walked all the way around this town." Rachel spoke in a soft voice. She didn't want to wake the Shaffers.

"I'm not tired. Are you?" Edward whispered too.

"A little." Rachel sat down on the bottom of the stairs and pulled Edward down beside her.

Edward put his arm around her shoulder and drew her close to his side. "We've covered all the basics, I think. Now we need to get to the important stuff. What's your favorite color, and what kinds of food do you like?"

Rachel tried to keep her laugh muffled. "By all means, we need the important things. What size shirt do you wear?"

They talked some, and sat in silence for long periods, enjoying the feeling of peace and closeness. Rachel covered her mouth with her hand and yawned.

"What time is it now?" Edward asked.

"Two. I can't believe the time is going by so fast. It feels like we just sat down here."

"Don't you have class in the morning?"

"Yes, and you have to go to work."

"Guess we better call it a night. When can I see you again?"

Rachel groaned. "I've got a lot of reading to do for one of my classes.

Tomorrow night, or should I say tonight, I'll have to read twice as much to make up for tonight. I know I won't get it done if you come over."

"I'm sorry." Edward moved his arm from around her.

"No, that's not what I mean. I won't want to do it if you're here." Rachel stood up and pulled Edward up. She put her arms around him and laid her head on his shoulder.

Edward held her close. "How about the next night? Friday."

"That would be great. I should be home by five but give me a little time to get ready."

"Get ready for what?" Edward teased.

Rachel leaned back in his arms and looked into his eyes. "Ready to talk some more and figure out who this mystery man is that's popped up in my life." She became serious. "This is a little scary, how I feel about you."

"I know." Edward sighed. "I'm going home now so you can go to bed. I'll try to stay away till Friday." He hugged her tight for a few seconds, then stepped back. He walked backwards for several steps, then turned and ran to the front of the house and down the sidewalk.

Rachel listened till she could no longer hear his feet hitting the concrete as he ran. She walked up the stairs slowly.

Am I dreaming all this? she thought.

Halfway up the stairs she stopped, turned around and looked back at the drive where Edward had vanished. A smile curled her lips.

He didn't even kiss me.

Edward ran until he was a block from his apartment. He slowed to a walk and tried to catch his breath.

Who is Rachel? I know her. I've held her in my arms before.

He stopped and turned around, and looked back down the street.

I didn't even kiss her, but I've kissed her many times. I know I have. This is crazy.

"Of course you have, Edward," Willow told his charge. "You aren't supposed to remember, but somehow you do. Someone is going to have some explaining to do. I'm glad I'm not in charge of erasing memory."

Thursday evening Rachel hurried up the stairs to her apartment. She was determined to get all the reading assignment completed that night.

Dinner would have to be a snack of what ever was in the refrigerator. She tossed her books on the couch and went to the bedroom to change clothes. Comfortable clothes would help her relax, and that would help her think.

Back on the couch in old lounging pajamas, she opened the book. Fifteen minutes later she put the book down and groaned.

"I have no idea what I've just read," she said in exasperation.

She went into the small kitchen area and put a pan of water on the stove. As the water heated, she put a tea bag in a cup.

Some caffeine should wake me up and make me think, Rachel thought hopefully, and poured the hot water into the cup. A knock sounded at the door. She dropped the pan, spilling the small amount of hot water remaining on the floor. She stood with both hands braced against the cabinet where her cup sat, waiting. The knock came again, softly. She hadn't imagined it. She took a deep breath, walked slowly to the door and opened it.

"I know I said I'd stay away until Friday, but I just had to see you. I'll only stay a few minutes." Edward's anguished expression said more than his words.

Willow turned his hands up and shrugged in a helpless gesture. "It was all I could do to keep him from hunting Rachel down in class today."

Aspen laughed. "You should have let him. I don't think she heard a thing all day. She thought these college classes were the most important thing in the world, after her parents died. I think her priorities have changed. Isn't it wonderful to see them together again?"

"Wonderful, yes. And if Edward will stay here a while, I can relax for a minute." Willow settled himself on the stair railing. "You wouldn't believe how many times I had to step in today to keep him from serious harm. He almost grabbed a 220 electrical wire before the breaker was disconnected. He walked right in front of a car that was speeding through a parking lot. That kind of thing went on all day. I need a second guardian to take shifts with me."

"Well, you can relax now. I don't think either of them will be going any where for a while." Aspen settled on the railing across from him.

Rachel opened the door wider and stepped back.

Edward came in and stopped in front of her. "I forgot to do something last night." Gently, he put his arms around her and drew her near, his eyes never losing contact with hers. He lowered his face as she tilted hers up. Both their eyes closed as their lips met.

Complete at last. They melted against each other. Each had a part of the other, and the belonging surged through them stronger than ocean tides.

Several minutes passed. The lost time was of no importance to Rachel and Edward, but they finally parted enough to again gaze into each other's eyes.

Rachel was the first to gain some control of her senses. She stepped one step back from Edward, took a deep breath, and grinned at him. "Well. I'm glad you dropped by." Laughter suddenly bubbled from her and Edward pulled her close again, also laughing.

Rachel gently pushed away from him, stepped to the side and pushed the door closed. It had been open since Edward walked in.

"Seriously, Rachel. I don't want to interfere with your studies. But... but I couldn't go another whole day without seeing you." Edward shook his head and ran his hand through his hair. "I sound like some kind of nut, don't I?"

"If you are, I'm keeping you company. I was just going to have a cup of hot tea. Want some?"

"Tea? Sure, if there's no coffee in the house."

"I've got coffee, too. I'll put it on. Sit down. It won't take but a minute."

Edward sat in a chair facing the kitchen area so he could watch her. He suddenly had a feeling that if he lost sight of her, she wouldn't really exist. She would be a figment of his imagination.

Rachel came back from the kitchen and chose a seat on the couch, facing Edward.

"It'll be ready in a minute." Rachel frowned and looked down at her hands before she looked back up at Edward. "I hope you understand that I've never acted like this before. Please don't think I throw myself at every new guy I meet. I can't explain what's going on between us, but I want you to know this is serious with me. I'm not just playing games."

Edward leaned forward with his elbows on his legs and his hands clasped together before him. "It's serious with me, too. Durn serious. This isn't a game."

He got up and moved to sit beside her. He took hold of her shoulders and turned her partially toward him.

"I'm going to say this, and I've never said it to a girl before. I love you, Rachel. I don't care if we did just meet. I love you with everything in me. I'm not much good at sweet talk, and I hope you can understand how important this is ... how deep this feeling goes in me. I guess I've waited all my life for you, and just didn't know it." Edward moved his hands from her shoulders and clasped her hands in his.

Tears came to Rachel's eyes, and her lips quivered as a smile curled up the corners. "Oh, Edward. I..."

The phone rang, sounding loud and unwanted. It rang twice more before Rachel pulled her hands from Edward and got up to answer it.

"Hello...

"Yes, Tom. I am busy...

"No, I already have plans for tomorrow night...

"You made yourself very clear the last time we talked. I don't think further explanation is necessary...

"You can call me next week, but don't bother making the trip this weekend...

"Yes, I'm serious...

"I don't want to get into that now. As a friend, you can call next week. Bye." Rachel hung up the phone.

Edward's brow drew into a look of concern as he studied Rachel still standing by the phone. She glanced at him, then looked down at the phone again.

"I'm causing problems in your life, aren't I?"

Rachel turned from the phone. Her eyes looked sad but she was smiling.

"I'll have to tell you about Tom." She sat back down on the couch by Edward.

"Tom is the first boy I ever dated in high school. Our parents arranged it. We became very close friends and have dated ever since then. But he wants something more than friendship, and I can't give him more." Rachel leaned back on the couch and crossed her arms, almost hugging herself. Confusion, guilt, and uncertainty washed through her.

Edward let the silence drag on for a while as he studied her face. The coffee could be heard hissing on the burner as it boiled from the spout of the pot. "I think the coffee's ready," he said.

Rachel got up and went to the kitchen. Edward followed her. She poured the coffee and added sugar to her cup. Edward declined the sugar, picked up his cup and took a sip.

"I drink mine black."

Rachel leaned against the cabinet. "I hope you understand about Tom. It really bothers me to think I'm hurting him. We are so close. When my parents died, I don't think I would have survived if Tom hadn't been there. I wanted to crawl in a hole and stay there. Tom was by my side and helped me do the things that had to be done. Mr. Gorman, my parents' attorney, tried to help. Well, actually he did help, but he could only advise. Tom was the one that made me follow that advice. Tom's so intelligent, and practical. I've always felt safe with him. Always knew he'd do the right thing. Now I feel mean and ungrateful because I can't be what he wants me to be. I can't return his love."

Edward studied Rachel's face. He couldn't see her eyes. She had kept her head down and looked at her coffee cup the whole time she talked. He reached out and put his hand under her chin, raising her face so he could see her eyes.

"If we hadn't met, could you have loved him the way he wants?"

"No. Oh, I don't know. I've never felt for him what I feel for you." A slight smile softened the anxiety that had been on her face. "There's never been any fireworks like ... like ..."

Edward put his coffee cup on the cabinet, took hers from her hand and sat it beside his. He slowly and softly pulled her into his arms. "Like this?" Their lips met.

The kiss was soft. Her lips parted under his. The softness vanished. Both strained against the other. Their tongues tasted, explored. Their hands on the other's back sought new places to hold, to feel. One of the coffee cups, full of coffee, was knocked to the floor and shattered. Neither noticed.

Edward broke away from the kiss. He pressed his face against Rachel's hair, his breath ragged. He tried to push her body away from his, but she clung tight and moaned softly.

"No. No, Rachel, honey. Not like this. Not now." He pulled her arms from around him and held her hands close to his chest.

Rachel looked at him with pleading and questions. She didn't want him to stop.

Edward took a deep breath. "Let's sit down, cool off, and talk about this. I don't want us to do anything that you'll feel bad about later. Okay?"

"Okay." Rachel stepped back and looked at the floor. "Guess I better clean up the coffee, too."

Edward grinned. "I'll help. Sorry your cup got broken."

They cleaned up the broken pottery and coffee. Rachel got another cup and filled it. She tasted of the one that still sat on the cabinet. It was sweet. She handed the new cup to Edward, and they went to the couch.

Several minutes of silence followed, interrupted only by the sound of the coffee being sipped. Edward sat his cup on the small table in front of them and turned to Rachel. She still looked straight ahead or down at her cup.

"Rachel, you don't have any idea how hard it was for me to stop what was happening. I'm going to be perfectly honest with you. If you were any other girl, just a date with some girl I'd picked up at the college, we'd already be in your bed. But you're not any other girl. You're Rachel. You're special. I love you. This thing between us has got to go just right. Am I making any sense?"

Rachel sat her cup down, too, and turned to him. Her eyes looked damp, on the verge of tears.

"I thought you stopped because you didn't want me."

"Didn't want you?" Edward pulled Rachel to him and put the side of his face against hers. "My God, woman! Couldn't you feel how much I wanted you?"

Rachel put her arms around him and began to rub his back as he nuzzled her hair and kissed her neck.

She sounded breathless. "I guess ... I guess I was so busy ... wanting you ... I wasn't ... thinking too clearly."

Against his will, Edward's lips found Rachel's again. Rachel slid back against the arm of the couch, pulling Edward with her. Desire engulfed them. The need to be one was beyond their control.

The phone rang ... and rang ... and rang. They broke apart. Rachel answered the phone, spoke briefly, and hung up.

She smiled timidly at Edward as she stood up and straightened her clothes.

"That was Mrs. Shaffer. She wanted to know if I could bring her a cup of sugar. She's baking something. It's hard for her to get up the stairs. I think she saw you come up here and she's just looking out for me."

Edward stood up, too. "I think the smart thing for both of us is for me to leave now."

"No." Rachel moved toward him.

Edward chuckled and put his hand out like a traffic cop. "Hold it right there. Mrs. Shaffer needs her sugar, and she needs to see me leave. Don't want to tarnish your reputation." He became serious. "If I stay we both know what's going to happen. I'm going home and take a cold shower. You're going to finish your homework. Neither of us will probably get any sleep tonight." He stepped forward, bent quickly, and kissed her cheek and stepped back. "I'll see you tomorrow." He went to the door before she could say anything that might change his mind.

"I love you." He was out the door and his footsteps sounded loud on the stairs as he hurried down.

Willow and Aspen had sat across from each other on the top railing of the stairs the entire time Edward was in Rachel's apartment. Willow patiently groomed a frayed feather that wouldn't stay in place.

"Do you ever wonder what it feels like to have a soul mate?" he asked Aspen.

"No. Not really. I know what my love for Rachel feels like, but I know soul-mate love is entirely different. It must be wonderful and excruciating at the same time. We've seen the pain it brings when something happens to one of them, and we've seen the indescribable joy they feel when they're together. I don't think my own soul could endure that much turbulence. I'm satisfied to let Them deal with human emotions."

Willow gave up on repairing the frayed feather and pushed his wing tip behind him. "But wouldn't you, just once, want to feel what they're feeling right now. Every guardian within a mile is probably picking up the waves of love coming from that room. It makes me tingle with happiness." He vibrated his wings and the leaves on a near by tree trembled from the unusual breeze.

Aspen smiled and pointed at Willow's wing where another frayed feather showed.

"You'd better stop doing that. It's rough on the wings, and they can't be replaced. Lose your wings and you'll end up with a desk job."

Edward came out of the door and brushed between the two guardians. Willow left his perch and floated down the stairs behind him.

"Looks like we're headed home. I'm sure I'll see you soon." Willow looked back at Aspen with a mischievous smile and vibrated one wing.

Aspen shook his head with a wry grin and turned to check on Rachel.

"Durn it, Dick. Isn't this day ever going to get to five o'clock? I feel like we've been working about twenty hours." Edward held the large bulletin board in place while Dick fastened it to the wall.

Dick continued to work without looking up. "Are you that tired? It's a little after four. You probably wouldn't be so tired if you'd gotten some sleep last night. I woke up a couple of times and heard you wandering around in the kitchen."

"No, I'm not tired. I just want quitting time to get here so I can see Rachel."

Dick finished putting in the last screw and turned to scrutinized Edward with a worried frown. "Man, you've got it bad. I never saw you go this ga-ga over a girl before. Have you already been to bed with her?"

Edward's eyes snapped with anger when he faced Dick. "She's not that kind of girl." He took a half step forward. "I have feelings for her I never had before. You're my best friend, Dick, but don't ever say anything bad about Rachel if you want to stay my friend."

Dick held up his hands. "Whoa. I didn't mean nothing bad. If Rachel's your girl, that's fine with me."

Edward felt a little ashamed as he turned and began to gather up tools. "Sorry, Dick. I know I'm acting nuts. You're right. I didn't get much sleep last night, but I really don't feel sleepy." He grinned at Dick as they started out of the room. "I've just got a bad sickness ... love sickness."

Dick swatted Edward on the arm. "Then let's get that last bulletin board put up before you lay down and die."

Rachel hurried across the parking lot to her car. Her smile touched everyone she met whether she knew them or not, and they had to smile back. The glow of happiness that surrounded her spread to all those around her and spirits were lifted. Today she didn't even mind carrying Toby's guitar.

She started the car and searched for a good radio station, something happy and smooth, something with love songs.

"Love me tender, love me true," she sang along as she drove out onto the street. There was only time for that song to play and another to start when she got to her driveway and pulled in. The smile left her face, replaced by a worried frown. Tom's car was there.

Rachel parked, turned off the motor and sat, gripping the steering wheel. She didn't want to see Tom now. She didn't want to think about the decision he would demand.

She took a deep breath. "No point is just sitting here," she said to herself. "Might as well get it over with."

She started up the stairs. Tom opened the door, met her a few steps from the top and took Toby's guitar from her.

"Mrs. Shaffer let me in like she always does. She certainly is a nice lady. I hope we can find a landlady as nice when we get our first place, after we're married." Tom went back up the stairs and waited at the top, holding the door open for Rachel.

Rachel stayed on the step she was on. Her brows were knit and her lips pursed.

"Tom! Didn't you hear anything I said to you on the phone?"

Tom put the guitar just inside the door and came back down the steps. He took Rachel's arm and guided her up to the top. When they were inside, he shut the door.

"I knew you must be upset about something else. And I should have waited to tell you the wedding plans when we were together. It was thoughtless of me to write it in a letter that way." He turned Rachel toward him and held her arms as he stepped forward and kissed her briefly on the lips. He stepped back and smiled. "I forget that girls like the romantic stuff. But never fear. This time, while I'm here, I'll do it properly ... on one knee, with the ring. Mother gave me great grandmother's ring to give you. It's quiet valuable, you know. You can wear it this weekend, but I think it would be prudent if I take it back with me and keep it in the vault until the wedding."

Rachel listened to Tom with her mouth open and her eyes wide. She couldn't believe what she was hearing. She turned from him, walked to her desk and put her book satchel on it. She looked back at him, shook her head and sat down in a chair.

"Tom, I don't want to hurt your feelings, but do you know how pompous you sound? I never noticed it before. A friend of mine called you a stuffed shirt, and you know what? You are."

Tom hurried to the couch and sat down facing Rachel. He looked worried as he leaned forward. "Rachel, honey, I know I'm doing this all wrong. You've known me long enough to know I do and say dumb things when I'm scared. And I'm scared now. I love you with all my heart. This being away from you all the time is horrible. I got the idea if we went ahead and got married, we could both continue our education and be together at the same time. That's all I want, Rachel ... to be with you all the time. It scares me to think about the responsibility I'd be acquiring, but I'll learn to deal with it."

Rachel sighed. "That's one of the problems. A marriage should be two people sharing responsibility. Do you honestly think I'll sit back with a lacy fan, sip tea and act like an old-fashion southern belle? I'll share my life with whomever I marry but he'll have to accept the fact that I've got a life of my own. I may want to have a career. I don't know what yet, but I may want to. A wedding band is a ring, not a chain."

Tom took off his glasses and rubbed his face, put the glasses back on and looked intently at Rachel.

"I understand all that. You can do anything you want until we decide it's time to have children. That's when my real responsibilities will start, as bread-winner and head of the house." Tom paused, then continued quietly. "Your parents expected us to get married. You know that's what they wanted."

Rachel gasped and her eyes filled with tears.

"That's not fair, Tom. I want you to leave. I can't ... I don't want to talk about this now."

Tom slowly stood up. "All right, I'll leave and give you time to think about this." He walked around the small table between them, bent and kissed Rachel on the cheek. "I'll come back in the morning. By then I'm sure you will have decided that I'm right." Tom went to the door, turned briefly with a confident smile, then left.

Rachel heard his steps down the stairs. She heard his car start. Then she was crying too hard to hear anything.

Why did he have to say that? Why did he have to bring my parents into this?

"But I don't love him, Mother. I know you said he'd take good care of me and our children. I don't want to be taken care of. I just want to love and be loved. I want Edward!" Rachel buried her face in her hands and sobbed. She didn't hear the repeated knock on her door or hear it open.

Toby stood in the partially opened door. "Rachel?"

When he got no response, he entered quietly, went to her side and knelt.

"Rachel? What's wrong? Are you sick or hurt?" He pushed her hair back off her forehead but couldn't see her face covered by her hands.

Rachel didn't answer him. In a few moments she got up, ran to her bedroom and slammed the door behind her.

Toby stood up. He was undecided about what he should do. He went to the bedroom door and listened. His own heart ached at the sound of her sobs. Rachel was more than just upset, and this was more than he knew how to handle.

"I guess I'll get my guitar and go on home now," he called at the door. "Call me if I can do anything. If you need any help ... or anything."

He got no reply. With his guitar in hand, he quietly closed the door behind him and left.

Aspen hovered close and stroked Rachel's hair. "Rachel, Rachel. You have to hear me. Open your heart and listen. Your mother understands. She knows about Edward and she's happy for you. Tom is a nice young man, but he's not for you. He's not your soul mate. You and Edward belong together. Please hear me, Rachel." Aspen knew part of her pain was about Tom but most of it was about missing her parents. Tom's words had broken open the partially healed wound in her heart put there by their loss.

Edward stood before his open closet with a towel around his waist. Four work uniforms shared the clothes rod with three shirts and two pair of jeans. A small pile of dirty clothes were on the closet floor. He pulled out a shirt, looked at it and put it back. He selected another and a pair of jeans. He hummed softly to himself as he dressed.

The humming stopped as a feeling of anxiety washed over him. He hurriedly pulled on his boots and started combing his wet hair as he walked to the living room.

"Hurry, Edward. Rachel needs you. She's hurting. Aspen can't get through to her. You must help her." Willow fluttered around Edward and pushed at his mind. Rachel's pain must be great to reach out this far.

"Dick, can I use your truck? I was going to walk to Rachel's but I've got a crazy feeling I need to hurry."

Dick laughed. He dug in his pocket and pitched the keys to Edward. "Yeah, I've had that crazy feeling before."

"No, it's not what you're thinking. I feel like something's wrong."

Dick stopped grinning. "Okay. Drive careful. I hope you're wrong about the feeling."

Edward hurried out the door. He drove over the speed limit all the way to Rachel's apartment and luckily didn't get stopped. The truck tires skidded when he stopped in the drive by the stairs. He took the stairs two at a time and opened the door without knocking.

"Rachel?"

There was no answer. He moved to the bedroom door and listened. He heard nothing.

"Rachel?" he said again as he opened the door.

Rachel lay across the bed with her face buried in her folded arms. Edward moved quickly to her side.

"Rachel? What's wrong, honey?" He tried to turn her over but she resisted.

"Go away, Edward. I can't talk to you now."

"No, I won't go away. Something's bad wrong and you're going to tell me what it is."

Rachel sighed deeply, rolled over and sat up. She reached for a tissue on her nightstand but found only the roll of toilet tissue. She pulled off several sections and blew her nose. When she looked up at Edward he could see her eyes were red and swollen. But worse than the redness was the look of total anguish.

"Honey, what's happened to get you this upset? Has someone died?"

Rachel pursed her lips. She wanted to hold in the words she knew she had to say.

"Tom was here when I got home."

"Did he hurt you? I'll have a talk with that guy. He'll never bother you again." Edward reached to pull Rachel into his arms, but she held back.

"No. No, you won't talk to him. He reminded me that my parents wanted him and me to marry. And I know he's right. If they were alive, still here giving me advice, they'd tell me to marry Tom and get this foolish feeling I have for you out of my head. I can hear my mother saying that as if she were here." Rachel gave one brief sob, breathed deeply, and looked away from Edward.

"You need to leave now. I won't see you again. I can't see you again."

After several moments of silence, Rachel turned and looked at

Edward. The look of shock and pain on his face tore another hole in Rachel's heart.

"Edward," she wailed. "Leave. Please leave. Now."

Edward stood up like a man in a dream. He backed slowly toward the bedroom door and stopped when he reached it.

"I love you. What you're saying doesn't make sense. Your parents are dead so you don't know what they'd say. I think Tom is a real bastard for using their memory to get what he wants. I'll always love you, and I'll be waiting for you when you come to your senses." Edward turned, straightened his shoulders, and very purposefully walked out and down the stairs.

Rachel lay back on the bed. The tears she thought were all cried out ran silently down the side of her face and into her hair. The pain was much like the pain of losing her parents. Tom had been there to help sooth that pain. Now Tom was the cause of it.

I wish I never had to see him again. Edward's right. He's cruel.

Rachel felt resentment building in her, quickly turning to anger.

No. I've got to stop thinking like that. Tom didn't mean to hurt me. He loves me. I know he does. He's only doing what he thinks is best for me. Everything will work out okay. I love him, in a way, and I'm sure I'll learn to love him as a wife.

Rachel turned over, buried her face in her arms again, and cried the unstoppable tears of pure agony.

Aspen and Willow had stood by helpless.

"Isn't there anything we can do to stop this horrible mistake?" Willow asked Aspen.

"I don't know." Aspen's voice resounded with the distress he felt. "I spoke with Tom's guardian while they were here. He feels it will make Tom happy to marry Rachel so he must help him accomplish that by whatever means necessary. A guardian's first obligation is to his charge. I couldn't argue against that."

Willow paced the floor. "But did you tell him about soul mates?"

"He knows about soul mates." Aspen sighed and tried to hover closer to Rachel. "He said sometimes they get parted, and he's right. This time was supposed to be different. I don't know what to do."

"Maybe you should go back for a meeting with Them. Ask Their advice." Willow had stopped pacing and hovered close to Edward, trying in vain to comfort him.

"I can't go off and leave Rachel now. You see the state she's in. Can you go?"

Willow followed Edward as he backed to the door. "I'll try. I'll have to get Edward settled down first. After he goes to sleep tonight, if he goes to sleep."

Then Edward was down the stairs and gone, followed by Willow.

Edward drove slowly, the window down, his left elbow on the door. He stopped at stop signs and red lights. He turned right for no reason, and left the next time. When he finally came to his senses, he was outside of town on a country road. He pulled to the side and turned off the engine. He rubbed his face with his left hand while his right stayed on the steering wheel.

This has been a bad dream. I'm just waking up. I've found Rachel, the only woman I can ever love. Nothing will keep us apart. I'll go to her apartment now and everything will be fine. It's just a bad dream.

He suddenly knew it wasn't a dream and leaned forward, resting his head on the steering wheel. The first sob erupted hard and painful.

"My God, Rachel! Don't do this to me. Don't do this to us." He cried. His body shook. He was lost in a world of pain he had never experienced in this lifetime.

Edward slowly raised his head and leaned back in the seat. The evening that had started with high expectations had settled into night, dark as the torment inside Edward. He took several deep breaths, then scrubbed at his wet face with both hands and transferred the tears to the legs of his jeans.

It's not going to end this way. I won't let that son of a bitch ruin our lives. Rachel doesn't love him. She loves me. I know, with everything in me, we're going to be together. I can't live without her. I won't live without her.

He started the truck and drove back to his apartment. He was calm now. He was settled and determined. Nothing was going to keep them apart.

Dick was not home when Edward entered the empty apartment. He went out to the small patio and sat looking into the night. After an hour of muddled thoughts, emotional exhaustion finally led him to his bed and a dreamless sleep.

Willow watched Edward until he was sure his charge slept deeply and soundly.

"I must leave you now, Edward, for a short time. This will be the first time we have been apart since your birth. Sleep well. I will try to find an answer that will mend the problems that keep you and Rachel apart. Be patient. They do not always consider the meaning of Earth time to humans."

Willow drifted reluctantly away.

Edward walked slowly in front of the Shaffer's house. He stopped at the edge of the drive. Tom's car was parked by the stairs. He took a hesitant step up the drive and stopped.

Willow gently pushed Edward back.

"No, Edward. Wait. It's not yet the time. Rachel's heart must have time to rest and heal. She is as unhappy as you but you can't stop that unhappiness now. It's for a reason. They said to wait."

Edward looked up at Rachel's door.

Will Rachel be angry with me if I go up there right now and confront Tom? Will it drive us further apart?

He turned, shoved his hands in his pockets, and with a frown, walked away.

I'm not a kid anymore. If I went up there now, I'd end up hitting the creep. I'll talk to Rachel alone. I've got to make her see she doesn't owe this guy anything. She doesn't love him. We'll work it out. We'll be together. I just have to pick the right time to talk to her.

Tom took his cup of hot tea to the front window of Rachel's apartment.

"It's a beautiful day, Rachel. When you finish those class assignments, we'll go out. A picnic in the park would be nice."

Rachel didn't reply or look up from the book in front of her.

Tom saw Edward on the sidewalk and tensed when he saw the hesitant step toward the apartment. He watched, with relief, Edward turn and walk away.

That must be the man Rachel thinks she's in love with, or so she tells me. I'll have to do something to keep him away from Rachel when I'm not here. I'll have the phone put in my name too, with a new number.

"While you're finishing your work, I think I'll run down and see the Shaffers. They're such nice old folks." Tom put his cup on the table, kissed Rachel's cheek, and went down the stairs.

Rachel stared at her left hand. Her ring finger burned as if being stung by ants. She scratched at it hard, almost bringing blood. Tom had taken the ring when he left but he would bring it back the next time he came, and she would have to wear it.

The instructor in the front of the room was still talking. Rachel hadn't heard anything he said. The board behind him was covered with notes and page numbers. She quickly copied the notes onto the page before her. Tom would be unhappy if she didn't pass this class.

"You must keep your grades up," he had told her. "We both will be proud of our accomplishments."

A buzzer sounded somewhere in the building and all those around her hurried or ambled from the room. She followed and stood uncertainly in the hall. She couldn't remember what her next class was, or where it was. She didn't live in her world anymore. She lived in Tom's. The hall was almost empty when routine took over and she walked toward the stairs that would take her to the next class.

"Please let your heart be lightened, Rachel." Aspen went with her *down the stairs. "This is only a small painful part of your life. Edward is still your soul mate. Don't let the free will of another stand in the way of the ultimate goal you and Edward asked for. You and Edward are to grow old together. Tom is not a bad person. He was a helpful friend when you needed him, but he is not the one you go through eternity with. He does not hold a piece of your soul. Be calm and wait." Aspen's words buffeted against the callus Rachel was building around her emotions.*

Edward watched Rachel leave the building and go to her car. She walked slowly with her head down.

Edward and Dick were in another parking lot across the shady lawn from Rachel. Dick reached for the 'reserved parking' sign Edward held. Edward had turned, putting the sign well out of Dick's reach.

"Wake up, Edward." Dick followed Edward's gaze. "Oh. Okay. Go talk to her. You're not any help here."

"No. There're too many people around. I'm going over to her house after work. I think that son-of-a-bitch Tom goes back to his school during the week."

Edward continued to watch until Rachel drove out of the parking lot and out of sight down the street.

Edward walked briskly up the drive and took the stairs two at a time. Rachel's car was parked by the stairs so he knew she was home. He knocked.

"Rachel?"

There was no reply. He tried the door and found it was locked. He knocked harder and shouted, "Rachel!"

A small voice came from below. "Young man!"

Edward turned and saw Mrs. Shaffer standing at the bottom of the stairs.

"I've come to see Rachel but something must be wrong. She won't come to the door, or maybe she can't. Would you let me in so I can check on her? She may be sick or something."

Mrs. Shaffer looked very stern at Edward. "Rachel isn't ill. Tom left instructions that she didn't want to see you or be bothered by you. Now I must ask you to leave and don't return or I'll have to phone the police." She crossed her arms over her chest.

Edward came part way back down the stairs. "Does Rachel know Tom told you that?"

Mrs. Shaffer's frown deepened. "Tom is an honorable young man. He wouldn't lie. Are you going to leave or do I have to phone and have you removed from this property?"

Edward came all the way down and stood facing the resolute old woman. "Okay. I'll leave. But you should ask Rachel if she really doesn't want to see me. And you better ask her today because I will be back."

Mrs. Shaffer stood silent and unmoving. Tom turned and left, walking tall with his shoulders back.

When he reached his apartment he went straight to the phone. Dick sat on the couch, drinking a beer and looking through the mail.

"You got a letter from your mom."

Edward nodded but continued dialing the phone. He listened for a moment, then slammed the receiver down.

"The number's no longer in service. He had the phone changed. That bastard thinks he's going to keep me away from Rachel. Well, he's wrong." Edward slouched on the couch, laid his head against the back, and looked up at the ceiling.

"Here's your letter. Maybe it will get you in a better mood."

Edward took the letter, tore it open and read. He finished and put it on the coffee table, but remained silent.

"What's the news from home?" Dick asked.

"Nothing much, really. Dad's had the flu but he's better now. Some neighbor shot another neighbor's cat. Now Mom's worried about hers. Pete just got another promotion. He's going to take the folks out for dinner to celebrate as soon as Dad feels like it." Edward leaned back and stared at the letter.

Dick took another drink of beer and sat it on the table, turning it idly in the circle of moisture that had dripped from the bottle. "Want to go get something to eat?"

"No. I'm not hungry. Is there any more beer in the frig?"

Dick stood up. "Yeah. I'll get us a couple."

Willow watched as Edward drank one beer after another. Dick left and returned with two burgers and more beer. Dick ate both the burgers and Edward drank most of the beer. Three hours later, Dick helped Edward to bed, pulled his boots off, and left him to sleep it off. Willow hovered briefly over the bed, noting the even breathing and soft snores.

"I must leave now and go speak with Aspen. Sleep well. The morning will find you with a headache, but it won't be the first time. Maybe someday I'll understand why you do this to yourself. Do you think the pain in your head will wipe out the pain in your heart? It won't. We're trying to help you. Give us time."

Aspen welcomed Willow. "I'm glad you came. Did you meet with Them?"

"Yes, and I still don't understand but I accept what They say. We must help Edward and Rachel as best we can. We're to comfort the two of them as much as possible. They say everything is as it should be. This is Tom's time to be happy."

Aspen gazed at the sleeping Rachel. "It's not for us to understand. I'm glad you spoke to Them. I hope Rachel and Edward will let us comfort them. She hasn't listened to me lately. She's too hurt and confused."

Willow began to drift away. "I know. Edward is the same way. I can't get through to him. Hopefully we'll soon know what They mean. The heartache needs to end."

The guardians parted. The problem was still there but They said it was as it should be. So it must be.

Dick shook Edward's shoulder. "Wake up, sleepy head. It's a work day."

Edward opened his eyes and shut them quickly. "Oh, Lord," he moaned and brought both hands up to his head. "Please tell me you have coffee made."

Dick laughed. "There's coffee and aspirin waiting for you in the kitchen. You pulled a good one last night. It may be a rough day but you might as well hit the floor and get it started."

"Okay. I'm awake. Thanks." Edward sat up on the side of the bed as Dick left the room.

Edward showered, letting the cool water hit him in the face. Feeling somewhat better, he dressed and went to the kitchen for the coffee and aspirin.

Dick finished a bowl of cereal, put the dish in the sink, and got another cup of coffee. "Did that beer last night give you any ideas about how to get your girl back?"

Edward poured his second cup. "I'm going back over there after work. She's going to talk to me. I'm just not going to roll over and give up." He stared morosely at the black liquid. "Dick, I love that girl. I never loved nobody like this. We belong together, and somehow, someway, we will be."

Dick quietly studied his friend. "Well, I hope it works out for you." He sighed deeply and stood up. "We better get going or we'll be late."

"Yeah. I'm ready."

Dick and Edward climbed into the truck and began their day.

Evening shadows covered the Shaffer's driveway as Edward pulled the truck in next to the stairs and parked. He sat for a moment, composing the words in his head that he wanted to say to Rachel. He stepped out and shut the door at the same time Mrs. Shaffer came out her back door.

"Young man, I told you not to come back here." Her small voice was strained.

"Yes, Ma'am, you did. And I told you I'd be back, and I am." He walked around the truck and went up the stairs. Mrs. Shaffer went back into her house.

"Rachel, you might as well come to the door. I'm not leaving till you hear me out." He knocked repeatedly on the door. "Rachel, I love you. If you don't love me, just come out here and tell me you don't, and I'll leave you alone. But I don't think you can tell me that because it's not true."

Edward heard a car pull into the drive and turned to see a police car coming to a stop behind the truck. Two policemen got out. Mrs. Shaffer came out her back door and walked over to them.

Edward turned back to the door with renewed knocking. "Rachel, you better come out. Mrs. Shaffer has called the cops on me."

Both policemen started up the stairs.

"Now, son, we just want to talk to you. I'm officer Terrell. There seems to be some problem between you and the young lady that lives here. So you just come on back down the stairs and we'll talk." Officer Terrell stopped a few steps down from Edward.

"No, sir, I can't do that 'til Rachel talks to me. Then I'll be glad to talk to you." Edward backed against the door and almost fell backwards when the door suddenly opened. He turned to face Rachel. Her eyes were full of tears that spilled over and ran down her cheeks.

"Please don't arrest him. I'll talk to him." Rachel stepped back from the door.

Edward looked at the policeman for permission. Terrell was chewing on his lower lip and Edward could tell the man was thinking of all the bad things that could happen.

"I promise I won't hurt her. I love her."

"Okay, son. You got fifteen minutes. We'll just wait out here to make sure this ends quietly." The two policemen went back down the stairs and joined Mrs. Shaffer who waited nervously by their car.

Edward stepped into the room and Rachel shut the door behind him.

"Edward, I told you I couldn't see you anymore. Don't make this any harder than it is already." Rachel pulled a tissue from a box, wiped her eyes and blew her nose.

"Rachel, look me in the eyes and tell me you don't love me and that will be the end of it."

Rachel turned away and wouldn't look at him.

"See. You can't do it because you do love me. I don't know what this Tom is holding over you but we can get around it. We belong together.

We'll get married, have a dozen kids and a great life together. Please, Rachel. Look at me."

When Rachel turned and gazed up at Edward, his heart sank. The look of hopelessness in her eyes said more than words could.

"I'm sorry Edward." Her words were little more than a whisper. "You don't understand. There are too many things from the past you can't understand. Go away and forget about me. I'll be marrying Tom this summer." She walked to the door and opened it.

Edward took a deep breath and fought down the tears that burned at his eyes. "I guess if that's what you really want, I'll have to go. But I'll never forget you. I'll never stop loving you." He went slowly from the room and down the stairs. He heard the door shut with a quiet click behind him. It was a small sound but it completed the breaking of his heart. He stopped for a moment and closed his eyes, then continued down and went to his truck.

Terrell let him get in the truck before going to stand by the open window. "What's your name, son?"

"Edward Neely."

"Well, Edward. I have a son almost grown, like you. I'm talking to you now as a father, not a policeman. Right now you think you'll never love another girl. You feel like the world has crashed down on you. Believe it or not, I was young once, and I know what it's like. Go home. The sun will come up in the morning like it always does. In time, you'll meet another girl and fall in love again. You don't think so now, but that's how this crazy life works. Don't come back over here causing problems. It won't do you any good, and you'll just end up in jail. Do you understand that?"

Edward brushed at the tears that wouldn't stay where he tried to keep them. "Yes, sir."

"Go on home now." The two officers got in their car and backed up, out of the way of the parked truck.

Edward backed out of the drive and drove toward his apartment. His rear view mirror showed the police car driving behind him. It followed all the way home, stopped and the officers watched until he entered the apartment.

Dick sat on the edge of the couch, leaning forward to look out the window. "Looks like you brought company home. Guess it didn't go too good."

"Nope, guess it didn't." Edward walked straight to his room and closed the door.

Rachel watched from the window until Edward drove away. She went to the couch and curled up in a ball on the end of it. The pain was too great for tears.

If this is the way I'm going to feel the rest of my life, I don't want to live.

Aspen tried hard to reach the pain in Rachel with no success. "Oh, Rachel. I tried to warn you about the pain that could come with having a soul mate. Why didn't you listen to me? Now you know. Now you feel it. But They assure me things are as they should be. We must accept that. Please be patient. Let me help you. Don't close your heart to me. Just wait and pray for comfort. Then I can give it to you." Aspen knew his words and feelings were not penetrating the wall of pain around Rachel.

The spring semester was nearly over. Rachel had thrown herself into the work but still her grades had dropped. She was still passing but only by a small margin. Tom's weekend visits had become regular. He spent the nights at his parents home twenty miles away, and all the days with Rachel. Every Friday evening he came with the ring for Rachel to wear until Sunday afternoon. She hated the ring and the symbol of what it represented.

I wish my finger would rot off so I didn't have to wear that thing. This is how the slaves must have felt in the old days when their owners put metal collars around their necks. I feel owned. I guess Tom does own me. And then we'll go through the wedding ceremony and the ownership will be complete. Oh, Mother. I wish you were here so I could explain to you how I feel. Maybe you'd understand. Or would you just make me feel guilty because I don't love Tom?

Rachel tensed when she heard someone bound up the stairs to the apartment on a Friday evening. Tom burst through the door without knocking.

"Good news, Sweetheart. I've made arrangements with the Herrings for you to stay with them this summer until the wedding. It's just down the street from my parents so we can be together all the time. Isn't that great?"

Rachel curled her mouth into a small smile she didn't feel. "Yes, that will be nice." She didn't move from her place on the couch where she sat with an open book in her lap.

He bent and gave her a quick kiss on the cheek before going to the desk. He leafed through the papers there and turned to Rachel with a frown.

"I see you still haven't brought your grades up. You know if you transfer to Rice with me in the fall, that isn't going to look good."

Rachel put a bookmark in her book and laid it on the table. "I'm sorry Tom. I can't seem to get my mind on my work. I keep thinking about the wedding plans."

A broad smile replaced the frown on his face. "Of course. I can't seem to get it through my thick skull that women think differently than men." Tom sat on the couch beside her. "I've got good news for that, too. Mother finally got a confirmed date for the church. Our wedding will be the first Saturday in August. And Mrs. Herring is giving us a wedding shower in July. You'll need to give her a list of the friends and family you want to invite. Mother needs a list, too, for the wedding."

"I'll be sure to do that." Rachel reached for her book.

Tom leaned back on the couch. "I need to talk to Mrs. Herring about the shower. It can't be the last weekend in July."

Rachel did not look up from the book she had opened. "Why not?"

"I received a letter from an old friend. He's going to be in Houston that weekend and wants me to come down to see him. I thought I'd also look around for an apartment close to the campus." Tom took the book from Rachel and put it on the table without marking her place. He put his arms around her and drew her against his side. "Thinking about our own place is exciting, isn't it?"

Rachel looked straight ahead. "I suppose. I haven't really thought about it."

Tom, very carefully and deliberately, placed his hand on Rachel's breast.

Rachel jerked upright and turned to stare at him. "What do you think you're doing?"

"I'm about to make love to the woman I love, to my fiancé. Rachel, we've dated for years. We've never been intimate. It's time to change that. I've read several books, and all of them say the act of physical love is something that has to be learned to be completely satisfying. You know the old saying, 'practice makes perfect'. If we start practicing now, we'll be perfect by the time we get married. It will make our honeymoon more fun. All the shyness and nervousness will be gone."

Rachel continued to stare at Tom. This is the man I'll be going to bed with for the rest of my life. He'll own my body and there's nothing I can do about it.

She took a deep breath. "All right Tom. If you think that's the right thing to do."

He smiled. "I've given it a lot of thought, and it's absolutely the right thing to do." He stood up, took Rachel's hands and pulled her to her feet. He started toward the bedroom still holding Rachel's hand.

Rachel tried to pull her hand from his grasp. "Wait, Tom. I don't think I'm ready for this. Please, couldn't we wait 'til we're married?"

Tom stopped and looked at Rachel with eyes that had turned cold and steely. "Don't question my decisions, Rachel. Have you ever known me to be wrong? Haven't I always given you correct advise?"

Tightness began to close around Rachel's throat. She tried to take a deep breath but it broke into pieces and her stomach jerked. Rachel looked down, unable to meet the look in his eyes. She whispered, "No. You're always right."

"Good." His smile returned. "Now, let's try to enjoy this." He led her into the bedroom.

"If it will make you feel more comfortable this first time, you can put on a nightgown or something," Tom said as he began to unbutton his shirt.

"Yes. Yes it would. Excuse me. I'll put it on in the bathroom." Rachel opened her dresser drawer and removed her long sleeved flannel gown. She took it into the bathroom and shut the door.

Her hands shook as she removed her clothes and slipped the gown over her head. She fastened the buttons close up under her chin. She looked in the mirror over the sink and turned away quickly. She didn't want to face herself or what was about to happen.

Tom was in bed under the sheet when she came out of the bathroom. His clothes were neatly folded and hung on a chair. Rachel walked to the side of the bed. The sheet on her side was folded back. She sat down and lifted the sheet to get in, and realized she still had on her socks. After a tiny hesitation, she got in bed and pulled the sheet up to her chin.

I've got my socks on so I'm not completely naked.

The socks made her feel more dressed than the gown did.

As soon as she was settled with her head on the pillow, Tom rolled against her. He raised on his elbow and kissed her. Rachel closed her eyes. The kiss was long but Rachel was unable to respond to it.

"Damn it, Rachel! Can't you kiss me like you did when we were in high school? You seemed to enjoy it then."

"I'm sorry, Tom. I'm ... I'm just nervous." Rachel kept her eyes closed.

When Tom kissed her again, he ran his hand down her body under the sheet and began to pull her gown up. It was tucked securely under her legs and did not come up easily. He ended the kiss and Rachel felt him throw the sheet off them. She closed her eyes tighter.

Rachel could feel the gown being pulled roughly and heard the material tear. The gown was shoved up almost to her chin. Tom moved close against her, and she realized he was completely naked. The hard maleness of him pressed against her hip. His hand clutched at one bare breast and squeezed painfully. His mouth was on the other, sucking and biting. Rachel clinched her teeth and held back the cry of pain lodged in her throat.

He moved his hand from her breast and shoved it between her legs without moving his mouth from her breast. Rachel tried to hold her legs close together but he pulled them apart. She could feel his actions becoming more frantic. He moved his mouth from her breast and put his head on her chest, his breath hard and gasping.

Rachel cried out when he pushed his finger into her. He didn't react to her cry, as if he hadn't heard it.

Tom suddenly sat up. Rachel opened her eyes when he began to pull her legs apart.

"No, Tom. Please stop. Please." Rachel hardly recognized the man that was crawling between her legs. He didn't look at her face. His glazed eyes focused on her pubic area. He grasped his engorged penis in his hand and moved toward her.

Rachel tried to move up in the bed, away from this man she didn't know. "No, Tom! No! Don't do this. Let me up."

He looked up at her then, with eyes hard and wild.

"Shut up, Rachel. Don't fight me. I've waited a long time for this."

He put his hands on her hips and pulled her back to him. He stretched out on top of her and she beat and shoved at his chest, but couldn't move him. Rachel had never realized how strong he was. Then he pushed into her. Rachel's scream was cut short by his hand over her mouth. He pushed again, and Rachel felt her body tearing. She tried to close her mind to the pain.

Rachel closed her eyes tightly. Tears seeped out and ran down her temples, into her hair. Oh, dear God, help me. Make him stop.

He moved in and out of her raw flesh rapidly a few more times, then collapsed on her with a guttural grunt. The weight of his body mashed her chest and she couldn't breath.

"I can't breath," she managed to gasp.

Tom slowly moved off her and lay on his back beside her. Rachel turned on her side with her back toward him, pulled her knees up to her chest, and released the sobs that tore at her heart. She felt his hand on her shoulder and flinched away. He patted her back.

"The books say it's always painful for the woman the first time. Next time it will be better and maybe you can enjoy it too. It was really great for me. Now I think I'll take a little nap. Why don't you take one too. Later we'll go out for dinner. A little celebration is in order, don't you think?" Tom patted her back again.

Rachel stilled her sops but remained drawn up in a tight ball. When she heard his breathing turn into light snores, she eased from the bed and went to the bathroom. She shut the door quietly and turned the lock. With the shower turned on hot, she pulled the gown over her head, wadded it up and shoved it to the bottom of the small trash basket. The water was too hot but she eased herself into it. She soaped her washcloth and scrubbed between her legs, ignoring the pain it brought back. The hot water ran out and turned to cold before she finally stepped out and dried off. The clothes she had taken off hung on the wall hook.

I still feel dirty. She put the clothes back on. She turned to the mirror. The face she saw wasn't her face. The eyes were red and swollen. Her lips were swollen. Her hair, damp from the shower, hung in twisted tangles.

That isn't me, she thought as she pulled a brush through the tangles. It will never be me again.

Aspen had tried to get passed Thistle, Tom's guardian, but he stayed between Willow and the bed.

"Thistle, let me get to Rachel. She needs me."

Thistle held his place, his hands out before him, palms up. "No, Aspen. This must be. Rachel will suffer no permanent harm. Tom has thought about and wished for this for years. Soon they will be married. This act today consummates that marriage before it happens."

Aspen fought against his hostile feelings and the temptation to knock Thistle aside. *"You can not make me believe this violent act that causes so much pain is right. I can not - I will not accept that."* He straightened out his hands when he realized they were balled into fists. *"There will be a report made to Them. If you value your position, you'll help me stop this."*

"No, Aspen. I think it would be best if you left the room now."

"I would feel her pain no matter how far away I went. The pain in her soul is as great as the pain in her body, or greater." Aspen heard Rachel's mental cry for help. The guardian rules of conduct could not stop him. He shoved Thistle roughly to the side and reached Rachel's side just as Tom rolled off her. He wrapped his arms around her as she lay in a ball. Her armor, completed by Tom's actions, blocked Aspen. She could feel none of his love and comfort. This thing Tom had forced her to endure, added to the loss of her parents, then the loss of Edward, had all combined to enclose a sea of futility and despair inside the fragile body of Rachel. Aspen felt all this, and was torn apart.

"My Rachel, my Rachel. I'm so sorry. I should have protected you better. I should not have let this happen."

Aspen raised his eyes when Thistle moved to his side and touched him lightly on the shoulder. Thistle looked sad.

"I'm sorry, too, Aspen, but we agreed to accept the free will of humans when we became guardians. There was nothing I could have done differently."

Aspen slowly released the anger that he had never felt before and nodded. *"I'm sorry I pushed you. But I will do the same thing if it happens again, only sooner. I don't know how I will stop it, but if Rachel cries out for help again, I'll be there. And there will be a report sent to Them about this."*

Thistle moved to the far side of the bed where Tom snored softly. Aspen continued to hold Rachel as her sobs quieted.

Edward and Dick sat on their patio drinking beer after work. They had worked outside most of the day and their uniforms were still slightly damp from perspiration. The patio was on the east side of the apartment complex and completely shaded by the building. A breeze added a cooling touch.

Dick was concerned about his friend. Edward had worked all week like a sleepwalker. The jobs had been completed with little or no conversation. Dick cleared his throat.

"Next week classes will be over for the semester. Then we'll really get busy. With the students out of most of the classrooms, any maintenance on those rooms has to be done. Summer semester is always a light attendance."

Edward didn't answer or comment.

Dick continued. "Why don't you take a few days off and go home for a visit? You have some vacation days coming."

Edward was still silent and didn't look at Dick.

"If the trip would cut you short, I can handle the rent by myself next month. You need to get away from here for a while."

When Edward still made no reply, Dick moved in front of him and sat on the edge of the brick wall.

"Listen, man. Rachel is history. You might as well get that through your head. She's going to marry somebody else. You didn't know her long enough to get this bummed out about it."

Edward tipped the bottle back for the last drink and sat the empty bottle on the patio beside his chair. "Yeah. I think a trip home would be good." He got up and started inside, but stopped at the door. "But you don't know what you're talking about when it comes to how I feel. I couldn't love Rachel more if I had known her all my life. It's like I've always loved her," he paused, "and I always will." Edward went inside.

Dick looked after him and shook his head.

I don't know whether to envy him or just hope it never happens to me, he thought.

The bus pulled into the station and Edward could see Pete waiting on the outside platform. Pete smiled broadly and waved when he saw Edward through the window. Edward pulled his small bag from the overhead rack and made his way slowly down the isle behind the other passengers. Two steps from the bus door Pete grabbed him in a bear hug and pounded his back in a brotherly fashion.

"It's good to see you, little brother." Pete stepped back, still holding both of Edward's arms.

Edward couldn't help but return Pete's grin. "Like wise, big brother."

They made their way through the Saturday evening bus crowd to the parking lot. Pete stopped by a 1957 yellow Chevrolet convertible. He threw the bag he had taken from Edward into the back seat.

Edward stepped back from the car and gave the admiring look and low whistle he knew Pete expected.

"When did you get this?" Edward opened the door and got in.

Pete got in and put the key in the ignition with a flourish. "Had her a week. Isn't she a beauty? The guy that owned her died in a hunting accident and his mother wanted to get rid of it fast. Seems she never did like it. I almost felt guilty taking it for what she was asking."

"Almost, but not guilty enough to offer more," Edward said with a crooked grin.

"I said guilty, not stupid."

The brothers laughed as they drove out of the parking lot. Pete maneuvered his sleek new car through traffic and drove to a small lake that was the town's water supply. He parked by a playground just as the sun dipped behind the trees on the far shore. He cut the engine off and turned to Edward.

"Okay, spill it. What brought you home? And don't give me any crap about being homesick or wanting to see us. Mom said you sounded funny on the phone, and I can see it in your eyes. You've got hurt written all over your face."

Edward looked away from Pete. He could feel tears building behind his eyes and his throat was tight.

"I didn't know it showed like that." Edward still could not look at Pete.

"It shows. You better get it out now or you'll break down in front of the folks like you're trying to do now."

Edward finally turned to Pete with a sick smile. "I'm in love. Big time. This isn't one of those crushes you saw me go through when I was in school." A tear broke through the fight Edward waged against it and trickled down his cheek. He brushed it away roughly. "I love Rachel with everything in me and she's going to marry someone else."

"Oh, Eddie," Pete moaned and put his hand on Edward's shoulder. He hadn't used that form of Edward's name since they were young. Then they had fought when he called Edward that, or Edward called him Petey. There was only love in the name now.

More tears rolled down Edward's face. He suddenly got out of the car and walked to a nearby picnic table where he sat on the bench seat.

Pete slowly followed and sat on the end of the table, facing away from Edward, toward the lake. Both were silent.

Edward gained control of his emotions and blew his nose. Pete left his perch and moved to sit across from Edward.

"So what are you going to do? Are you moving back home?"

Edward didn't answer right away. That idea had been one of many going through his mind. "No. It would be dumb to leave my job. There's not much work for me here." He held his hands out across the top of the table. "I finally got all the grease out of my hands and that wouldn't last long back here. I like it down there. The winters sure beat the ones here. And I keep hoping Rachel will come to her senses and get away from that jerk she's engaged to. I know she loves me. He's got some kind of hold over her I don't understand."

Pete got up, walked around the table and stood behind Edward. He put his hands on Edward's shoulders.

"I was hoping that, if you had a problem, I could help you with it. But this is way out of my league. I can make sure you don't have time to sit around and mope about it while you're here. I'm taking a few days off too. We'll find something to get into."

Edward reached up and put his hand over his brother's. "Thanks, Pete."

Tom parked his car and went up the stairs to Rachel's apartment. He opened the door without knocking and called, "Rachel."

"In here, Tom." She answered from the bedroom.

Two sealed boxes sat by the front door and two more were open on the kitchen cabinet. Tom went to the bedroom. Rachel was removing clothes from the dresser drawer and packing them in a suitcase on the bed.

He went to her side and kissed her lightly on the cheek. "Hi, Sweetheart."

Rachel glanced at him with a quick smile and continued packing.

Tom sat on the edge of the bed. "I'm going to miss our weekends here. While you're staying with the Herrings, we won't have the privacy we had here. But we still have tonight and tomorrow night. I told Mrs. Herring we'd be there sometime Sunday."

And maybe I can get you pregnant this last weekend here, he thought. Then I won't have to worry about you trying to back out of the wedding.

Tom watched her go from dresser to suitcase with an unchanging solemn expression. "Aren't you excited about this? It puts us just a little closer to the wedding date."

Rachel stopped and looked at him. The smile she gave him came and went so fast, he couldn't be sure he really saw it.

"Of course, I'm excited. I'm a little sad, too. The Shaffers have been so good to me. I'll miss them. And I'll miss my apartment. This was my first home by myself. I wasn't here very long, but there are a lot of memories here." Rachel resumed packing.

Tom watched Rachel make another trip to the dresser and grabbed her when she was by the bed again.

"That can wait a while, can't it? I haven't seen you in a week, and it's been a long week. I've missed you." Tom tried to pull her down on the bed beside him.

Rachel put both hands, still holding articles of clothing, against his chest and pushed herself out of his grasp. "No, it can't wait. I have a lot to do. I told Mrs. Shaffer I'd be out tomorrow and have the place cleaned up good so the new tenants can move in Sunday. You better call Mrs. Herring and tell her I'll be there a day early." Rachel sounded impatient and almost angry.

Tom watched her make another trip that filled the suitcase. She snapped it shut and opened another one in its place.

I'd better not upset her, or make her mad, he thought. That would mess up my plans for tonight.

"Is there anything I can do to help?"

"You can go get us something for dinner and bring it back here."

"I'll do that." Tom got up and started from the room, but stopped at the door and turned back smiling. "Instead of me calling Mrs. Herring, we can just stay in a motel tomorrow night and arrive at her place when she's expecting you."

Rachel's reaction surprised and startled him. She threw the clothes she carried on the floor and turned toward him. "I feel cheap enough as it is. Now you want to take the chance of someone seeing us check into a motel, and really smear my reputation just so you can ... do ... whatever it is you want to do." Rachel turned away from him and wrapped her arms around herself.

Oh, god, I've done it now, he thought. "No, no, Sweetheart. I was just ... thinking about Mrs. Herring. How ... how it might ... make it easier on her." Tom stammered out the explanation. He wanted to go to Rachel and take her into his arms, but was afraid to.

Tom was not happy with himself. He felt out of character. Ever since that first time he made love to Rachel, he was unsure of himself. His main objective in life now, it seemed, was to make Rachel happy and keep her happy. His old confidence was gone. His grades had slipped. How could he keep his mind on his studies when the feel of her body under him was all he could think about?

He had even thought, Rachel was right. We should have waited until we were married. But that was a moot point now. What was done was done and he couldn't regret it. His desire for Rachel was almost to the point of desperation and obsession. He would do anything to keep her in his possession.

"Sorry, Sweetheart. I guess I hadn't thought about all that. I'll call Mrs. Herring after I get back with the food. I won't be long." Tom left and went down the stairs. A smile came back on his face when he got in his car.

At least we'll have tonight.

Edward got up from the kitchen table and took his empty coffee cup to the sink. "Well, I've got to get going if I'm going to catch that bus."

Pete got up too. "Wish you didn't have to go. Are you sure we can't talk you into staying longer?"

Edward smiled. "If I want to keep my job, I've got to get back to Texas."

Honey and Bobby remained seated. Bobby leaned back in his chair and looked up at his two boys. "I know how that goes. I'm glad you've got a good job to go back to."

Honey hadn't said much all morning and now sat looking at her half full cup of coffee. "You know you're welcome to move back home any time you want to."

Edward stepped to her side and leaned down to hug her. "Thanks, Mom. That means a lot to me." He stood up but kept his hand on her shoulder. "If things ever get too tough for me to handle, I'll take you up on that." He turned to Pete. "Ready to go?"

"Any time you are."

The family filed out of the kitchen. Edward picked up his small bag as they went through the living room. Honey and Bobby followed them out to the front porch. Edward hugged them both and hurried to Pete's car so they wouldn't see the tears running down his face.

"We love you," Honey called and waved as they pulled out of the drive.

"I love you too," Edward answered out the car window. He pulled a handkerchief from his pocket, wiped his eyes and blew his nose. "I've turned into a regular cry baby on this trip," he said to Pete as they drove toward the bus station.

"You've had something to cry over. Guess I'd do the same thing if I were in your place. Do you know what you're going to do now?"

Edward sighed and slouched further down in the seat. "Not anything for me to do. I'll go back to Denton, work, and hope Rachel comes to her senses."

"Keep in touch when you get home. You have my number. Call collect if you need to."

"Thanks, Pete, but I think I can afford a phone call once in a while."

They reached the bus station just as the bus was loading. There was no time for a long goodbye. They hugged by the bus door. Edward got on, and they looked at each other through the window for a brief moment before the bus pulled out.

Edward settled back in the seat to get comfortable for the long ride ahead of him.

Maybe I should think about moving back. If Rachel stays around Denton, or comes back to school there next fall, I'm bound to run into her. I don't know how I'll handle that.

He closed his eyes and drifted into the half sleep the swaying bus ride induced.

"Have faith, Edward," Willow consoled. "There is much we don't know, and more we don't understand."

Rachel found herself being very thankful when she parked behind Tom in front of the Herring's home. She didn't know these people, but they represented protection. Here Tom couldn't come to her bed and violate her again and again as he had done in her apartment. The sex was not as painful as it had been the first time, but it still left her sore and uncomfortable. She felt dirty all the time and bathed often, two or three times a day. She had learned to take her mind elsewhere while Tom got his satisfaction from her body.

Tom got out of his car and ran back to help Rachel with her luggage. He pulled the two suitcases out and Rachel picked up one of the boxes.

"Why don't I take those boxes to my house?" Tom said. "They'll just crowd your room here."

"No, I'll keep them with me. There are things in them I'll need." Rachel pushed the door shut with her knee and turned to the house.

Tom went ahead of her to the front door. The door opened before he got to it, and an older woman with a friendly smile stood waiting.

"Welcome, Rachel," Mrs. Herring said and stepped back to let them in. "We're so happy you'll be staying with us. We've heard so much about you, we feel like we know you." She shut the door behind them. "Your room is right down the hall this way." She led them into a comfortable bedroom. "We want you to make yourself at home. Over here is your own bath. If I've forgotten to put anything out you need, just tell me."

Rachel sat the box in a corner. "Thank you, Mrs. Herring. I really appreciate this. I could have stayed in my apartment in Denton but Tom wouldn't hear of it."

"No, of course not, Dear. This young man wants to keep you close. And I can see why." Mrs. Herring turned to Tom. "She certainly is a pretty thing."

Tom smiled. "Yes, ma'am, I think so."

Rachel blushed. "Thank you."

All of Tom's possessions are pretty, or expensive. Maybe if I got ugly he'd let me out of this engagement. Rachel instantly felt guilty for her thoughts, and turned away to hide her deepening blush.

"This is a lovely room." She went to the bed where Tom had put the suitcases. "Tom, if you'll bring in the rest of my things, I'll unpack."

"Sure, Sweetheart."

He left the room and Mrs. Herring moved to the dresser and opened the two top drawers.

"I've cleaned this out so you should have plenty of room to put your things. Do you need help with that?"

"No, ma'am. I'm just going to unpack my summer clothes. No need to do the winter ones."

"That's right. When winter gets here you'll be Mrs. Tom Gaines, and you two will be in your own place. We're all so excited about the wedding. Tom's mother talks of little else. She's hoped for this for years, ever since Tom was in high school. You know, she was a friend of your mother's. It nearly broke her heart when your parents died."

Rachel was placing clothes in the dresser while Mrs. Herring talked. At the mention of her parent's death, tears welled up in her eyes. She continued to move the clothes around, trying to push down the pain and tears. She soon realized she was fighting a losing battle. The tears were going to come.

"Excuse me," Rachel muttered and started for the bathroom.

"Oh, my dear. I'm so sorry. This must be hard for you without your parents here to share this happy time with you. It was thoughtless of me to bring it up."

Rachel was in the bathroom with the door shut, but she could still hear Mrs. Herring.

"I'll go on with my work in the kitchen now. Dinner is at seven. I'm making something special for you. I hope you like it."

Rachel buried her face in a towel to stifle the sobs. She could hear Tom and Mrs. Herring talking in the hall but couldn't make out what they were saying. She really didn't care.

Tom called to her through the door. "I've brought the rest of the boxes in. Is there anything else I can do?"

Go away and never come back, Rachel thought. She tried to keep her voice steady when she answered him.

"No, everything's fine. I'm just tired. Why don't you go on home. We can talk later."

"Okay. Mrs. Herring invited me for dinner so I'll see you then."

"All right."

Rachel sat on the closed toilet and let the tears come. Mother, why aren't you here now? Why did you go off and leave me? If you were here I could make you understand that I don't love Tom. I know you want me to marry him. You told me that enough times, but you didn't know I'd meet Edward. I'll marry Tom, just like you want me to, but I'll never stop loving Edward.

Rachel's tears finally stopped. She went into her bedroom, got fresh clothes from a suitcase and returned to the bathroom. She turned on the shower as hot as she could stand it and got in. She bathed roughly with soap in the almost blistering water and got out. She still felt dirty.

I guess I'm dirty under my skin and that won't wash off.

She dressed and finished putting her clothes away before she went to the kitchen to offer help to Mrs. Herring with the dinner.

Aspen hovered close to Rachel. Her sadness brought wave after wave of sadness over him, drowning them both in a tidal pool of desolation.

"Rachel, will you ever hear and feel me again? The wall you have around you keeps me out. But worse, it keeps all your pain in. Please have faith. You and Edward are special. We don't understand now, but someday, surly we will. Everything is for a reason. Trust and wait."

Edward sat on the patio with his coffee and watched the early dawn creep over the landscape. He had been going to bed earlier and earlier since his returned. Sleep brought blessed relief from the gnawing pain of loss in his heart. His dreams of Rachel were all good. Only there in his dream world could he find peace and happiness. Only there they were together.

He checked the time on his watch. I don't need to wake Dick for another half hour. Time for another cup of coffee.

Edward didn't eat breakfast anymore, choosing instead to fill up on black coffee. The slight bitterness of the strong brew seemed to match his constant mood. His appetite for lunch and dinner was poor too, and he had lost weight. He worked hard during the day, seeking the tiredness that would bring sleep. Dick had begun to complain that he couldn't keep up with Edward's constant rush in the summer heat.

Edward went in to wake Dick. He put his empty cup on the cabinet and picked up the two letters he had put there the night before. His mother and Pete wrote every week. Pete had called twice. A small smile twitched the corners of Edward's mouth. It helped a little just knowing his family was there if he needed them.

The family would love Rachel, Edward thought, and went on through the apartment to Dick's bedroom.

"Time to rise and shine. We're burning daylight," he called at the door.

Dick groaned, rolled over and looked at his clock.

"My alarm will go off in fifteen minutes. I don't need you crowing at me this early." Dick pulled the sheet over his head.

"You complained yesterday that you didn't have time to enjoy your breakfast. Get up now and you'll have plenty of time." Edward didn't wait for an answer. He returned to the kitchen and poured another cup of coffee. Dick would be lucky if he got one cup out of the almost empty pot.

Edward glanced at the calendar on the kitchen wall. It was still on June. He took it down and turned it to the next page. It was the first day of July. I haven't seen Rachel in over a month. The thought brought a twist to his gut.

Dick came into the kitchen wearing just his underwear and reached for a cup and the coffee pot. The cup was only partially full when the pot dripped the last drop. Dick yanked the pot plug from the socket.

"If you're going to drink all the coffee before you wake me up, make another pot." Dick opened the cabinet and rummaged for the coffee.

"Drink what you've got. I'll make some more." Edward moved to the cabinet and Dick took his coffee to the table.

Dick took a drink, put the cup on the table, and rubbed his face with both hands. "Sorry if I sound grumpy. I had crazy dreams last night and kept waking up. Guess it was that sauerkraut we had for supper. Funny but I can't remember what the dreams were about now. When I would wake up, I'd remember them real clear."

Edward plugged the coffee pot in. "Better eat wieners and sauerkraut in the middle of the day from now on."

"Yeah." Dick drank more of his coffee. The silence in the kitchen was broken by the blub-blub of the perking coffee. "I wish I could remember those dreams, though. They were weird. Not scary, just weird."

Willow and Spruce, Dick's guardian, enjoyed the early morning on the patio. They waited for their human charges to complete the morning activities.

"It seems you got through to him but he doesn't remember the message," Willow said.

Spruce looked perplexed. "I've never tried to deliver a message that's for someone else. I only succeeded in confusing Dick. Since he and Edward are such good friends, I was hoping he would pick up on it right away and tell Edward the 'dream'. I'll try again tonight and be more specific."

"Thank you. I've tried everything I know to get through to Edward. He won't ask for help with his pain and he pushes me away every time comfort is offered. It will be a relief when this situation is resolved and we can all understand the reason for it." Willow plucked idly at a frayed feather in his usual manner while gazing into the kitchen at Edward.

"Are you questioning Their reasons?" Spruce asked in alarm.

"Of course not." Willow paused for a moment and grinned. "Well, maybe a little."

Spruce snorted a slight chuckle. "I'm surprised you haven't been sent back for retraining or stuck behind a desk. When I think of all the things you have done through all of Edward's life times that were completely against the rules ..." Spruce shook his head and turned to watch the sun make it's way over the trees by the parking lot.

Dick and Edward worked on the west side of a building, repairing a window. They tried to get all the outside work done in the morning hours so they could retreat into the cooler interior jobs when the afternoon heat broiled down. A car pulled into the parking lot close to them and two young women got out. They were dressed in shorts, and both were tanned and attractive. "Hey, Dick," one of the girls called.

Dick turned and smiled. "Hey, Carol."

Edward tightened the last screw holding the window in and turned too. He knew Carol. She and Dick dated occasionally.

"This is my friend, Betty. Betty, this is Dick and Edward."

Dick smiled at the petite blonde standing by the dark haired Carol. She returned the smile shyly.

"Excuse us for not shaking hands, Betty." Dick held his dirty hands out, palms up. "As you can see, we're working men. What are you girls up to today?"

"Just stopped by to see if we're still on for the forth of July, and to see if Edward could join us. Betty came up to spend the holiday with me, and I thought we could make a real party out of it."

"Sounds good to me." Dick turned to Edward. "How about it?"

Edward looked at the ground. He didn't want to meet Dick's gaze. "I don't know. I'd really planned on ..." He glanced up and caught Dick's expression of warning. "Okay. Sure. Why not?"

Carol beamed. "Great. Betty and I will pack a picnic and we can go to the lake. Do you think we can all get in your truck or do I need to take my car?"

Dick stepped to Carol's side and put his arm around her, pulling her against him without touching her with his dirty hands. "I think the truck's a good idea. The closer the better." He grinned.

Carol returned his grin and swatted his chest. "Oh, you." She moved from Dick's grasp. "We've got to go now. There's a swimsuit sale we've going to check out. See you the fourth. Around ten?"

"Yeah, that will be great. Glad to have met you, Betty."

Edward remembered his manners. "Me too ... glad to meet you." He knew he didn't sound sincere and regretted it. "See you the fourth."

Betty looked embarrassed. "Sure." She turned and walked toward the car, and Carol hurried after her.

They watched the girls drive away, Carol waving out the window.

Edward began to gather up their tools. Dick leaned against the building and lit a cigarette.

"You're a real ladies man, aren't you?" Dick's tone was sarcastic.

Edward stopped his actions and looked across the parking lot where the car had driven from sight. "Sorry. I wasn't ready for that. I feel like it would be cheating on Rachel to date another girl."

Dick pushed away from the building and threw his cigarette on the ground. "Shit, Edward!" he said with disgust and bent to retrieve the remaining tools. He stomped toward the work truck with Edward close behind. "Rachel's planning to marry someone else. She's probably already sleeping with him, and you feel like it's cheating just to go on a picnic with a girl. I think it's about time you woke up." He threw the tools in the back and got in. Edward did the same and remained silent.

Dick stopped the truck before he reached the parking lot exit and hit the steering wheel with his fist.

"Damn it, Edward. I'm sorry you lost your girl but you can't keep moping around like you have for over a month now. Living with you has been like living with some cranky old woman. I'll tell you the truth. A few times I felt like knocking the crap out of you." He drummed his fingers on the steering wheel and stared straight ahead.

"The fourth of July we're going to pick the girls up and go to the lake. You're going to be nice to Betty and act like you're having a good time or, so help me, I will knock the crap out of you." He finally looked at Edward and a slow smile changed his expression. "You scared?"

Edward rubbed his hand over his face in a gesture of abashment and returned Dick's smile with a crooked grin. "Scared to death."

Dick chuckled and drove out of the parking lot.

Edward leaned his arm on the open window. "I guess I have been a pain in the butt lately. Don't worry about the fourth. I'll have a good time if it kills me. I don't want you hurting yourself trying to whip me"

Edward was glad he had a friend like Dick.

Rachel reclined on a chaise lounge in the shade of the patio cover. She closed the book she had been reading and smiled wistfully as she thought about the story the book told. College studies had left her little time for pleasure reading. Mrs. Herring had directed her to the public library a few blocks from the house, and Rachel had become a regular visitor there. She could get lost in the lives of the fictitious characters that lived on the printed pages and briefly leave her own heartache behind in the real world.

She stood up and stretched. I'm getting lazy, she thought.

Life at the Herring's was comfortable and relaxing.

If I didn't have to deal with Tom, I'd feel like I was on vacation. Think I'll walk to the library to return this and get another one. It's not noon yet so it shouldn't be too hot and I need the exercise.

Rachel went to her room and got her purse. On the way out, she smiled and waved the book at Mrs. Herring, who was talking on the phone. Mrs. Herring smiled and waved back in acknowledgement. She understood where Rachel was going.

Rachel had easily fallen into the habit of telling Mrs. Herring where she was going when she left the house, just as she would have her mother. She had grown fond of the Herrings in the short time she had been in their house. Mrs. Herring loved reading as much as Rachel, and they often spent hours talking about books. They discovered they had read many of the same ones.

After many uncomfortable evenings with Tom's parents, Rachel couldn't help but wish they were more like the Herrings. Mrs. Gaines could talk of nothing but the wedding, and Mr. Gaines hardly talked at all, preferring to keep his head buried in the financial section of the newspaper.

The residential street was deserted as Rachel strolled down the sidewalk by the manicured lawns on the way to the library. A slight breeze kept her from being too hot in the rising temperature.

It will be a scorcher by this afternoon. I'd better find a book quick and get back to the air conditioning.

The sound of a truck brought Rachel to a halt. It sounded like Dick's. She turned and watched with disappointment as the truck drove slowly by her and stopped a short way down the street. Two men got out and removed a lawn mower and other yard tools from the back of the truck. Rachel began her walk again, and smiled at the two gardeners when she passed them.

What would I have done if it had been Edward in Dick's truck? Would I have gone with him if he stopped and asked me? Stop daydreaming.

It won't do any good. I'm doing the right thing. I'm doing what Tom wants. I'm doing what Mother wanted. I wish the right thing would stop hurting so badly.

In the quiet coolness of the library, Rachel paused just inside the door and took a deep breath. She loved the smell of libraries. All those books, some new and some a little musty with age, combined to tingle Rachel with the anticipation of pleasure. She handed the book she was returning to the smiling lady behind the front desk, and headed for the fiction section.

Aspen hovered in Rachel's path. It was urgent that he change her direction. "I've received a message for you Rachel. Since it's about books, I hope you'll hear me. I don't understand the message but it must be important to come to me this way from Them. Turn into the non-fiction section. Just look until you see the right books. The information they contain will be of interest to you somewhere in the future."

Rachel glanced up at the sign on the end of the shelves. Non-Fiction. She started to go on by, but something almost like a push turned her into that aisle. She looked down at the floor to see if something had tripped her. Seeing nothing unusual, she shrugged and began to look at the books.

A green dust jacket caught her attention, and she pulled the book out. The cover was a green mountain scene. She opened it and read some of the inside cover. It was about the state of Kentucky, some of the history and current day happenings. She flipped to the middle. There was an interview with an old resident of the mountains. She was soon caught up in the story. When that segment ended, she closed the book and tucked it against her. She wanted to read the rest of this one. A little farther along the shelves, a smaller, brownish, paperback book caught her attention. Canning, Quilting, and Other Mountain Arts. Without thinking, she placed it with the other book and walked to the desk to check out both of them.

On the way back to the Herrings she pulled the smaller book from under her arm and looked at it. What possessed me to get this? She thought. I've never wanted to can or quilt. Oh, well. It never hurts to read about new things.

When she came in sight of her current home, she saw Tom's car parked in front. Her steps slowed involuntarily and she swallowed, trying to force down the anxiety that rose in her throat. All too soon, she was at the front door, opening it, and stepping inside.

Rachel entered the foyer. She could hear Tom and Mrs. Herring talking in the living room. She took a deep breath, put a smile on her face, and entered the room.

Tom jumped to his feet and came toward her. "Hi, Sweetheart. You've got some more reading material, I see." He bent to kiss her and she turned her cheek to him.

"Yes. Mrs. Herring is spoiling me. I'm catching up on all the fun reading I didn't have time to do at school." Rachel put the books on the coffee table and sat on the couch next to Mrs. Herring.

Tom picked up the books, read the titles, and frowned. "Are you planning on us moving to the mountains?"

"No, of course not. They just looked interesting to me."

He put the books down but remained standing and smiled broadly. "We're going out to dinner tonight. There's a nice place in Dallas I want to take you to. Dress up pretty. Maybe we'll catch a movie after we eat if there's anything good showing."

"What time should I be ready," Rachel asked with resignation.

"Around seven. Maybe you should take a nap this afternoon. We may be out late if we see a movie." Tom moved to stand in front of Rachel and bent to kiss her. She turned her cheek to him again. "Well, I'll let you ladies get on with your day. Mother has some chores she wants me to help her with. I'll see you at seven."

Rachel made the corners of her mouth turn up. "Sure. See you then."

Tom left and the women sat quietly on the couch until the sound of his car faded.

Mrs. Herring turned slightly to face Rachel. "I don't mean to pry, honey, but is everything all right between you and Tom? You don't seem very excited about the wedding. In fact, a lot of the time, you seem sad."

Rachel looked at her hands, clasped in her lap. "Things are okay, I guess. I just thought ... I hadn't planned on getting married until after I graduated. I hadn't planned ... actually I hadn't planned on getting married for a long time. I know my mother wanted me to marry Tom, but . . .." Rachel stopped. She couldn't bring herself to voice her true feelings to Mrs. Herring who was, after all, friends with Mrs. Gaines.

Mrs. Herring reached for Rachel's hands and clasped them together in her hands. "Rachel, all brides start getting doubts before the wedding. This is extra hard on you because you don't have your mother here to confide in. If you can, put me in the place of your mother. Talk all your doubts out. Then you can start to enjoy the preparations for your big day. Your bridal shower is next weekend. Do you have something special to wear for that?"

Rachel smiled at the caring woman. "Thank you. You have made me feel very much at home here, just like my mother would have. I hadn't thought about what I'd wear at the shower. I probably should get something new for it."

"Tomorrow we'll go shopping. I want to buy you a really pretty dress for this occasion. And we'll have lunch while we're out. Let's make a day of it."

Rachel scooted closer to Mrs. Herring and hugged her. "Thanks. That sounds like fun."

Mrs. Herring patted Rachel's shoulder. "It will be fun. Now let's have a bite of lunch. Then you can take that nap Tom suggested."

Tom picked Rachel up at seven sharp.

"You're beautiful, as usual. Ready to go?"

Rachel answered with a small smile and followed Tom to the car. He drove toward Dallas, grinning over at Rachel occasionally and humming softly to himself.

Rachel frowned when Tom drove into a dirty, slum-like part of town. "Where is this place we're going to eat?"

"Right here," Tom said and pulled into the parking lot of a filthy looking motel. "I've got the room until midnight. There's some wine and cheese waiting so you won't go hungry."

Every muscle in Rachel's body tensed and she pushed herself against the back of the seat, as if that would somehow keep her in the car.

"No, Tom. I don't like this. It's cheap and degrading. And dangerous. Look at this place."

Tom turned in the seat, reached out and softly stroked Rachel's cheek. He suddenly grabbed her jaw and yanked her face toward him.

"Listen, sweetheart. I've been without you for as long as I'm going to. I'm headed for Houston next week and I'm going to have a good memory to take with me. You may as well relax and enjoy it. I'm going to."

Tom got out of the car and walked around to open Rachel's door. She got out and followed him into the room.

The sun was hot on the sandy beach and all the shade trees were surrounded by the early arrivals. Dick and Edward had anticipated that. They fastened one side of an old sheet they had brought to the side of the truck. They pulled long metal poles from the back, stuck them in the ground, and tied the loose corners of the sheet to them. They laughed at the sagging make-shift tent but it served its purpose. Carol and Betty spread a blanket on the ground under the shade and sat on it.

Dick grabbed Carol's hand and pulled her up from the blanket. "Let's swim. I want to see if that suit looks as good on you wet as it does dry."

Carol laughed. "Okay, okay. Come on Betty. Let's all get wet."

"In a minute. You go ahead. I want to check the lunch things." Betty pulled a box to her side and began to move things around in it. When Carol and Dick were in the water and out of hearing, she turned to Edward. "I know Dick had to drag you here today, and I'm sorry. I want you to know you don't have to entertain me or anything." She paused a moment and studied Edward who sat quietly looking down. "Carol told me you just broke up with your girl. That's a miserable feeling. I know because I'm just getting over a break up. If you want to talk about her or anything, I'm a good listener."

Edward took a deep breath and looked up at Betty with a relieved smile. "Thanks. And I'm sorry my feelings are so obvious. I promised Dick I'd have a good time but I guess I didn't tell myself that."

Betty laughed. "Well, you didn't promise me so you can be as unhappy as you want to when Dick's not around."

They were both silent for a while and looked out at the lake. Dick and Carol were splashing and playing among the other swimmers.

Edward leaned back on the blanket and propped himself up with his elbows. "Her name is Rachel. I think I fell in love with her the first time I saw her. She felt the same about me. I know she did. But she's tied up with some guy from her past, and he has some kind of hold on her I can't understand. Anyway, she left Denton with him when the semester was over and I don't know where she went. She may be married to the son-of-a-bitch by now. I know I should put her out of my mind ... just forget I ever met her, but I can't. I know I'll never be able to feel about another girl the way I feel about her." Edward scooted his elbows to the side, lay on his back and stared at the sheet flapping in the breeze above him.

Betty lay back and turned on her side facing Edward. "If you really feel that strongly about her, maybe you two are soul mates. And if you are, you shouldn't give up hope because you'll get back together ... somehow, someway, sometime." Betty turned on her back and watched the flapping sheet also. "I haven't met my soul mate yet. Some people never do."

Edward thought about Betty's words. Is she right? he thought. Is Rachel my soul mate? After several minutes, he became aware of the sweat soaking his body and sat up.

"It's hot. Let's go get wet." He jumped to his feet and reached down for Betty's hand.

"Sounds good to me," she said laughing, and let Edward pull her to her feet.

Willow settled on the top of the truck and watched Edward and Betty run into the water. Bean Pod, Betty's guardian, sat beside him.

"Thanks," Willow said. "I've been trying to get that message though to him for over a month. Your Betty is very receptive and very nice."

"Yes she is," Bean Pod agreed. "When I heard of your problem, I was sure we could help. It took a little work to get her here to deliver the message, but we did it."

"I can feel Edward's soul opening up again with hope. Maybe now I can get through to him again."

Bean Pod nodded. "I'm sure you can."

"Rise and shine. It's another work day." Edward sat a cup of coffee on Dick's bedside table and pulled down the sheet that covered Dick's head.

Dick blinked and frowned. "Don't be so cheery this early in the morning. It can't be time to get up yet."

"Look at your clock. You stayed out too late last night. Where did you and Carol go after you dropped off Betty and me?"

"None of your business." Dick rolled over, looked at his clock and groaned. He raised up on one elbow and reached for the coffee. "Thanks."

"Sure. I'm having some cereal so get your butt up and join me."

Edward went to the kitchen, poured milk on his cereal and began to eat. Dick followed in a few minutes, yawning and stretching.

"I haven't seen you in a good mood in weeks. You and Betty must have hit it off." Dick got a bowl and spoon and joined Edward at the table.

"Betty? Yeah, she's a nice kid, and we did have fun yesterday. But that's not the reason I feel so good. I had fantastic dreams all night about Rachel. We're going to get back together." Edward looked over at Dick with a grin. "Don't look at me like I'm crazy. I don't know when, but somehow It's going to happen. I'm as sure of it as I am of my own name."

Dick shook his head and gave Edward a skeptical grin. "Maybe I should start calling you Charlie or Goober."

"You might as well write it on the wall because it's going to happen."

Willow and Spruce smiled at each other and watched contentedly. No words were necessary.

Rachel slipped the filmy dress over her head and enjoyed the soft feel of it as it floated down her body. She fastened the buttons down the front of the bodice and stepped in front of the full-length mirror on the closet door.

Mrs. Herring spent way too much money for this, but it's the prettiest dress I ever owned, Rachel thought. Just wish I were wearing it for some other reason.

"Rachel, dear," Mrs. Herring called from the hall. "Are you about ready? The guests will start arriving soon."

Rachel opened the bedroom door and smiled. "Well, what do you think?" She swirled around and the fabric fluttered around her knees.

"Oh, my!" Mrs. Herring clapped her hands together and brought them to her chest. "You're an absolute angel. I hope Tom realizes what a prize he's getting."

Rachel tried to keep the smile on her face. "I guess I'm ready. Do you need any help with the refreshments?"

"No. The caterer Tom's mother uses took care of it. I wanted to make everything myself, but she insisted. All you have to do now is sit in the living room and look beautiful." Mrs. Herring moved close and put her arm around Rachel as they walked down the hall. "I'm truly going to miss you when you leave. I feel like I'm losing a daughter."

Rachel hugged Mrs. Herring. "You'll always be special to me. Now, if we don't want my makeup completely ruined with tears, we'll go in the living room and talk about this later." Rachel could feel the tears gathering on her lower eyelids, threatening to pour over.

Mrs. Herring quickly pulled a tissue from her pocket and softly blotted them away. "You're right." The doorbell rang. "Okay? Then let's go see how much loot you can haul in at this shower."

"Mrs. Herring!" Rachel tried to sound shocked, but dissolved into laughter.

Mrs. Herring joined her and they made their way to the front door together.

Rachel was emotionally drained. Her cheeks ached from the artificial smile pasted on her face. She sat on the edge of the couch and pretended to admire the silver tea service before her on the coffee table. Tom sat beside her with his arms outstretched on the back of the couch. He had arrived shortly after the last guest left. If she leaned back and relaxed, he would put his arm around her shoulder. She didn't want that.

Mrs. Gaines beamed proudly. The tea service was a gift from her. She had been the first to arrive. The shower was over now and only she, Tom, Mrs. Herring, and Rachel sat in the living room.

"I know you children won't need that right away," Mrs. Gaines said, "but after Tom gets established in his career, you'll be entertaining frequently. A good tea service will let people know right away what kind of home they're in, and what kind of people they're dealing with. You have to put your best foot forward to compete in today's world."

"It's very beautiful, Mrs. Gaines." Rachel put the cream pitcher she was holding back on the tray. "Everything we received tonight is really lovely. I certainly wasn't expecting all this." Rachel gestured toward the table at the side of the room that was covered with gifts. "Tom, did you look at everything when you got here?"

"No. I'll see everything when we use it."

"Would anyone care for more tea or coffee, and there's plenty of cake left," Mrs. Herring offered.

"Oh, no dear." Mrs. Gaines stood up. "It's getting late, and this has been a busy day. I think I'll run on home. Rachel, I'll come back tomorrow and help you get started on the thank you cards. You know it's good manners to do that right away."

"Thank you. I'll appreciate the help."

If they don't get out of here soon I'm going to lose it, Rachel thought.

This smile is on its last leg. My whole face is going to crack and my chin fall off any minute now.

Mrs. Gaines started to the door, then stopped and turned. "Tom, I know it's a short distance but I'm really tired. I walked down here and planned to walk home. Would you mind leaving now and give me a ride home. You need to be up early tomorrow anyway to start your trip to Houston."

"Sure, Mom." Tom pulled Rachel back against the couch and kissed her quickly. "I'll say bye now and not wake you in the morning. You can get your beauty sleep." Tom looked at his mother and Mrs. Herring and smiled. "Even though she doesn't need to be any more beautiful."

The women laughed.

Tom turned to Rachel. "I'll be back in four or five days. Then it will almost be time for our wedding."

"Have a nice trip," Rachel said, "and tell you friend hello for me. I've got plenty of new books to read while you're gone so there's no need for you to hurry back."

Tom stood up and laughed. "I'm almost getting jealous of books. Sometimes I think you'd rather have a stack of books around instead of me."

"Don't be silly, Tom. I just enjoy reading. That's all."

After a few more parting words and goodnights, Tom and Mrs. Gaines left. Mrs. Herring shut and locked the door behind them and returned to her chair.

"I don't know about you, Rachel, but I'm exhausted. It was a lovely shower, though, wasn't it."

Rachel smiled her first real smile of the night at Mrs. Herring. "I'm a little overwhelmed by all the gifts. A lot of those things are really expensive. I do want to get the thank you cards out right away." Rachel paused and looked at the smiling woman across from her. "How will I ever be able to thank you? I don't think a card will cover that."

"My dear, the pleasure I've gotten out of you being here is more than enough thanks." Mrs. Herring stood up. "Now, why don't we go to bed and leave this mess until tomorrow."

They started from the living room and stopped when sounds were heard coming from the kitchen.

Rachel laughed. "It sounds like Mr. Herring feels it's safe to come out of his den now and sample that left-over cake."

"Yes, I'm sure he was waiting for the sound of the door lock. He has very selective hearing. If I ask him to help with a household chore, he goes stone deaf. But he knew when the last guests left."

Rachel and Mrs. Herring hugged and parted in the hall. Rachel gratefully entered her room, shut the door, and slipped off her shoes. She stood quietly for a few seconds breathing deeply.

I want to lie down on that bed right now, Rachel thought, but if I don't undress and hang this beautiful thing up, I'll end up sleeping in it.

She put her clothes away and slipped into her pajamas. After cleaning the makeup from her face, and running a brush through her hair a few times, she crawled into bed. The sheets felt cool and crisp.

Tom's gone for a few days and won't be bothering me, Rachel thought. I've got a couple of good books to read. The bridal shower is over and done with, thank God. I can relax and enjoy myself for a little while. I can even think about Edward if I want to, and I want to. I've kept myself from thinking about him and I really don't know why. Just thoughts won't be cheating on Tom.

Rachel turned on her side and reached the lamp switch. In the sanctuary of darkness, she settled her head into the soft pillow. She only had to whisper his name and Edward was there, smiling and reaching out for her. She happily drifted into his arms and into sleep.

"You're up early this morning," Mrs. Herring said when Rachel walked into the kitchen. "I thought you might sleep late after all the excitement of last night."

Rachel smiled as she got a glass from the cabinet and poured herself orange juice from the container on the table. "I had a very good nights sleep. I feel all rested. Mrs. Gaines didn't say what time she'd be here today to help with the cards. I want to shower and dress before she gets here."

"I'm sure you'll have plenty of time. Would you like some breakfast now?"

Aspen's happiness was great and his extra glow obvious when he came into the kitchen with Rachel.

Mimosa, Mrs. Herring's guardian, greeted him warmly. "You certainly are beaming today. Is Rachel hearing you again? That's the only thing I can think of that would make you this happy."

"Yes, I spoke with her all night. She soaked up my assurance like a

sponge." A small frown suddenly dampened Aspen's look of happiness. "I have a feeling things are about to turn around. I still don't know how or what the final outcome will be for everyone. I'm afraid there will be some who will feel great sadness when things change, as they must. I'm truly sorry for the pain humans feel in the course of their lives. We're told it's sometimes necessary but I can't help wishing it wasn't."

Mimosa softly caressed the edge of Aspen's wing in friendship. "You do your job well. That's all that's important."

"Just a minute. I'll ask him." Dick put his hand over the mouthpiece of the phone and turned to Edward. "Carol says Betty is coming up this weekend. How do you feel about a double for dinner and a movie?"

Edward shrugged and looked back down at the magazine he was reading. "Sure. Why not?"

"Yeah, he thinks that will be great. We'll pick you up about six. Okay?" Dick listened for a few minutes before he laughed. "Well, you know what they say . . . birds of a feather. See ya', Sweety. Bye."

Dick walked around the couch and flopped down in the chair across from Edward. "You like Betty. Right?"

Edward put the magazine down. "Sure. I already told you I think she's a nice kid."

"Do you think you could get to like her a lot?"

"What's this about, Dick? You know how I feel about Rachel. If you're asking could I learn to love Betty the way I love Rachel, the answer is no. Betty could easily become a good friend, but that's all."

Dick grimaced and looked away from Edward. "Carol thinks Betty is getting a crush on you. She had a messy breakup with some guy in Dallas so it's probably just rebound." He looked back at Edward. "But how are you going to handle it?"

"I know about the breakup. She told me about it at the lake. I think you and Carol are making a lot more out of this than there really is. Let's see how tomorrow night goes. If it looks like she's looking for more than I can give, I'll let her down easy. That's all I can do."

Dick was silent for a while with creases of concentration on his forehead. He suddenly shook his head and stood up. "Women. All that stuff is way too serious for me. Let's go get something to eat."

Rachel curled up in the big leather chair in the den and opened the book at the bookmark, about in the middle. It was too hot to read outside today. Mr. Herring was at work, and had offered the use of his den for her reading comfort.

The picture on the page was a log cabin with green mountains rising all around it. The back of the cabin appeared to be on stilts; long logs keeping it level on the side of the mountain. Rachel studied the picture with delight. She had taken her time going through this book. The printed information was good but the pictures were fascinating. She had never been to Kentucky, and still didn't know what had made her pick this particular book. A determined thought had begun to build as she read further and further into the book. Someday I'm going to Kentucky.

Carol's car was more comfortable for the four of them than Dick's truck. She and Betty had arrived a few minutes late to pick up Edward and Dick.

Dick turned to look at Edward in the back seat. "Women never stop to think about their men waiting for them, starvation just around the corner. I don't know if I'll still have the strength to walk into the café. If I don't make it, you'll bring something out to me, won't you?"

Edward reached over the seat and patted Dick's shoulder. "Sure I will. But I may have to wait 'til I've eaten, to build up my own strength. Can you wait that long?"

Carol glanced at Dick with a menacing look. "Just keep it up, you guys, and I'll drive 'til I run out of gas. Then we'll drag your starved carcasses out and dump you at the side of the road."

Betty put her hands over her mouth and tried to stop the giggles that bubbled out but was not successful. Carol laughed, unable to maintain her mean look.

Dick grabbed his stomach and groaned. "I'm not kidding."

Carol pulled the car into a parking space in front of the café. "You're too late. We're here. You'll have to starve some other time."

Dick immediately sat up straight and grinned. "Okay."

Once inside, the food was served quickly, and they ate with obvious appetites and lively conversation. Betty had been offered a job in Dallas and Carol was trying to talk her out of it. Jobs versus college degree brought them close to an argument.

After the meal was finished, they still had an hour to kill before the movie. Carol drove to a nearby park. It was almost empty except for an old couple sitting on one of the park benches.

"Where are all the kids?" Dick questioned. "There are usually dozens here."

"Probably home eating supper," Edward guessed.

Carol ran to one of the swings. "Come swing me, Dick."

Edward and Betty sat on a bench. The sun was low and the temperature very warm, but the heavily wooded park offered a shady haven.

Edward relaxed with his arms spread across the back of the bench. One was behind Betty, and he patted her affectionately on the shoulder.

"The job offer sounds great. If you're happy about it, don't let anyone talk you out of it."

"Thanks, Edward. Carol has really nagged me about this ever since I got here and told her. You know, she'll probably go on through and get her teaching degree, but that's not what I want."

"You're lucky you know what you want. I've never given any serious thought about what I want to do in the future. This job I've got now is fine, but it's just a job."

They sat quietly for a while and watched Dick push Carol in the swing. She squealed and begged him not to push her so high.

Betty finally asked, "Have you heard from Rachel?"

Edward moved his arms from the back of the bench, leaned forward and put his elbows on his knees. "No. I guess I should try to forget about her. Dick nags at me about that just like Carol does you about your job. But I can't quit thinking about her. I've thought a lot about what you said that day at the lake . . . about soul mates. If only that was true."

It was Betty's turn to put her arm across Edward's back and pat him on the shoulder. "It still may be true. Sometimes things have to take their time to work out right. Don't give up yet."

"Thanks Betty. I need to get your phone number so I can call you when I start feeling down about this."

"Sure. I'll give it to you when we get back to the car."

Edward grinned. "Do you mind calls in the middle of the night? That's usually when it gets bad."

Betty laughed. "Why don't you just write it all down then, and call me the next evening before ten o'clock. We'll stay friends a lot longer that way."

"Friends, but under certain conditions. That sounds good to me."

Edward noticed Carol was no longer screaming. Dick was pushing her in the swing normally, and they both looked toward Edward and Betty.

Edward leaned back on the bench again. "Did you know Dick and Carol think there's a romantic thing starting with us?"

"Yeah, I get that from Carol all the time, how you've got a thing for me, and I need to get over my x."

Edward grinned. "Want to give them something to talk about?"

"Sure. What?"

Edward put both arms around Betty and slowly pulled her to him. He took a quick peek toward the swing. Carol had stopped swinging and Dick stood behind her. Both were staring. He kissed Betty slowly and deliberately. When he released her, she put her head against his neck. He could feel her shaking and was worried maybe he had taken the joke too far. Then he realized she was laughing.

Betty whispered. "Are they looking?"

"Yes."

"Well, don't let go of me yet 'til I can stop laughing. Sorry, Edward, but my first-grade boyfriend shook me up more than you do."

"You just don't know a good thing when it happens," Edward said. "I'll have you know, I was the class Casanova from the first through the fifth grade." He fought down laughter.

The whispers continued until Betty said it was safe to pull apart. Edward leaned back again with his arm still around Betty's shoulder. Betty burst into open laughter beside him and pointed at Carol and Dick. The couple seemed frozen at the swing. Dick's mouth hung open. Edward gave in to his laughter, stood up and pulled Betty to her feet.

"I think they're in a trance. Let's go wake them up."

They ran across the park holding hands like the children Edward had decided they would be.

Rachel flipped through the pages of the book, pausing now and then to look at the pictures one more time. She had finished reading about Kentucky and the book would be due at the library in a few more days. The craft book had been interesting and there were several things she'd like to make someday when she had time.

I'll take these back to the library this evening when it's a little cooler outside, she thought. Tom's due back from Houston sometime today. I hope he gets in too late to go out. I'll have to go to bed with him soon enough after we're married. I don't want another visit to that sleazy motel.

The phone rang in another part of the house and Rachel heard Mrs. Herring answer it. The conversation was muffled by the rooms between them. Rachel didn't pay any attention to the phone calls here. Mrs. Herring had many friends and the phone rang often. Tom or the Gaines were the only ones who would call her here.

Rachel continued leafing through the book, comfortable in Mr. Herring's big leather chair in the den. She became aware of Mrs. Herring standing silently in the doorway looking at her. She was very pale and leaned slightly against the door facing.

Rachel quickly stood up. "What's wrong? Are you ill?"

Mrs. Herring brushed her hand over her face. "Oh, Rachel. I don't know how . . ."

Rachel hurried to her side and took her arm. "Come sit down. Can I get you a glass of water?" She guided Mrs. Herring to the couch and helped her sit down.

Mrs. Herring grabbed Rachel's hand. "Sit down with me, dear. I have to tell you something, and I don't know how." Tears pooled in Mrs. Herring's eyes and spilled down her cheeks.

"Well, just tell me." Waves of anxiety washed over Rachel. She knew something very bad had happened to upset Mrs. Herring this way.

Mrs. Herring turned on the couch and reached for Rachel's other hand. She grasped them and brought them to her wet cheek. She took several ragged breaths, and lowered Rachel's hands to her lap.

"That was Tom's aunt on the phone."

Rachel gasped. "Has something happened to Tom's mother?"

Mrs. Herring looked down at their hands, and seemed unable to meet Rachel's gaze. "No. No, dear." She finally raised her face and looked into Rachel's eyes. "Tom's been in an accident."

"Oh, my God. How bad is he hurt?"

"Rachel," sobs shook the words. "He'd dead."

A cold tingling shock rushed through Rachel's body. She waited for the pain – the pain she had felt when she heard of her parent's death. It didn't come.

I know I'm supposed to act some way, she thought. What should I say?

Mrs. Herring released Rachel's hands and grabbed her shoulders.

"Rachel, I'm so sorry. I can't imagine how you must feel. What can I do? What can I say?"

Rachel sat stiff and silent. A feeling of relief tried to edge into her mind.

No, I mustn't feel that, she thought. I have to feel grief. Damn it, where's the grief, the tears? I have to say something. Tom's mother! Yes, I'll ask about his mother.

"You said his aunt called." Rachel's voice sounded robotic in her own ears. "Where is his mother? How is she?"

Mrs. Herring pulled Rachel into her arms. "You precious girl. Thinking of someone else when this must be more than you can bear. They had to call in her doctor. He sedated her and she's in bed. Do you want me to call him for you? I'm sure he'd come. He's an old friend of the family."

"No, really, I'll be okay. I . . . I need to be alone for a while. This doesn't seem real. I'll wake up in a little while and this will have been a dream . . . a nightmare." Rachel's words were halting. She pushed away from Mrs. Herring and stood up. "I'll just go to my room and lie down for a little while." She walked half way across the room, stopped and turned back. "That way I'll be in bed when I wake up." She started from the room again. "Yes, alone for a little while."

The sounds of Mrs. Herring's sobs faded as Rachel moved through the house toward her room. She closed her bedroom door and, for the first time since she'd been there, locked it. She went to her bed, sat on the edge and took several deep breaths.

Tom is dead. There won't be a wedding. I'm free. But I loved Tom in a way. I didn't want him dead, did I? He was my security. Mother wanted me to have security. I'm sorry, Mother. I can't marry Tom now like you wanted.

Those thoughts unleashed a torrent of pain, insecurity, fright, and self-pity. Rachel heard an almost animalistic moaning howl and didn't realize it issued from her own throat. The sobs followed. She fell back on the bed and curled into a ball. All the months of silent grief for her parents burst forth. The hard shell of self-reliance she had built around herself crumbled. The childish feelings she had suppressed for so long washed over her.

Mother I need you. I need you and Daddy. I don't want to be grown up yet. You left me alone and I don't know how to take care of myself alone. Now Tom's gone too.

Aspen hovered close over Rachel emitting all the comfort he could.

"Everything will be all right now, Rachel. Tom will understand what he did wrong. He didn't mean to harm you. His actions were just the misdirected love he had for you. Because of that love, he wants you to be happy. Both he and your mother want you to go to Edward now. With Edward you will grow and learn. You both will grow and learn."

Rachel's sobs lessened. She heard her name being called and knocks on her door, and realized it had been going on for a while. She sat up.

"Just a minute." She pulled several tissues from the box on her bedside table, wiped her face and blew her nose. When she opened the door, Both Mr. and Mrs. Herring stood there.

"We were so worried, Rachel. Please don't lock us out at a time like this. We want to help you." Mrs. Herring reached out and softly grasped Rachel's arm.

Rachel looked passed her to Mr. Herring standing quietly in the hall. She had never seen such a look of sadness and concern on the face of this normally easy-going man. The fact that he was there registered in Rachel's mind.

"What time is it?" she asked. "Is it time for you to be home?"

"No. Bea called me at work." Mr. Herring looked up and down the hall as if physically searching for the right words. "What can we do to help you?"

"I don't know. I'm sorry, but I don't know what I'm supposed to do right now, or say, or anything. Can you tell me what I'm supposed to do?"

Mrs. Herring let go of Rachel's arm and patted it. "You can come to the kitchen and we'll all have some hot tea or coffee – whichever you prefer. No decisions have to be made right now. We just want to help you get through this. We've lost people we love and know you don't need to be alone right now. Later, when you feel like it, we'll go with you to the Gaines'."

"Yes, some coffee would be good. Thank you. Thank you for everything. I'm lucky to be here with you."

Mrs. Herring led the way into the kitchen. "I don't believe it was luck that brought you to us. Sometimes God just puts us where we're supposed to be."

The next three days wound around Rachel in a blur. The Herrings thankfully guided her through. She had cried with the Gaines and for the Gaines. She had cried alone and with Mrs. Herring. Only she knew how many of the tears came from her own confusion.

She and the Herrings rode to the church, and later to the cemetery in the limousine furnished by the funeral home. The early afternoon heat at the cemetery was stifling, and Rachel welcomed the coolness of the big air-conditioned car on the ride back to the Gaines'. There was food and more tears. Rachel tolerated being hugged and cried over by total strangers. She found it very difficult to hide her relief when Mrs. Herring said they needed to get home so Rachel could get some rest.

The funeral is finally over, Rachel thought as the three of them walked towards the Herring's home. Maybe tomorrow I'll start thinking clearly again, and can figure out what I'm going to do.

The sunset turned the clouds in the evening sky pink, then orange. Rachel paused on the sidewalk in front of the house and looked at it. Mr. Herring unlocked the door and went in, but Mrs. Herring turned to see where Rachel was.

"You should come in now, dear. I know you're exhausted." Mrs. Herring walked the few steps back to stand by Rachel and look at the sky.

Rachel took her arm. "Isn't it beautiful? I was just wondering if Tom asked for this sunset for me so I'd know he was all right."

"What a lovely thought." Mrs. Herring was silent a moment. "Yes, I think that's probably exactly what he did."

The two women stood with their arms linked and watched the clouds slowly change colors with all the beautiful hues a sunset can have. When all the colors were gone, and only the evening sky remained, they went in the house.

"Would you like something to eat, Rachel? I noticed you didn't eat anything at the Gaines," Mrs. Herring asked.

"No, thank you. I'm not very hungry right now. Later maybe, if that's okay."

"Well, I'd like a cup of hot tea. Come have one with me. Then you can eat whenever you get ready."

"Thanks, but I'd just like to lie down for a little while. I'll eat later."

"Of course, dear. Let me know if I can get you anything."

In her room, Rachel undressed and slipped into a robe. She stretched out on her bed with a grateful sigh.

I'll rest a minute, then join Mrs. Herring for tea. Tomorrow I'll start returning all the gifts. I need to get everything done so I can get back to Denton. My apartment is gone so I'll have to find another one. Maybe there's a vacancy in Edward's building. Edward. Have you missed me as much as I've missed you? I'll be there soon, my darling. Soon.

Rachel's eyes closed. With thoughts of Edward, she drifted softly into sleep.

Dick put the paintbrush on the edge of the can, pulled a rag from his back pocket and wiped sweat from his face.

"Dang, it's hot. Let's do something where it's cool this weekend."

A few feet away, Edward applied paint to a window frame and didn't look up from the job. "Yeah. Maybe a movie. Double feature."

"Carol said Betty called. Wanted to know if we were doing anything this weekend. She might come up."

Dick worked for a moment in silence, waiting for a comment from Edward. When none came, he continued. "Betty's a nice girl. I'm glad you two are getting along so good."

"Yeah." Edward's answer was noncommittal.

"Maybe we can go out to the lake again. That was fun." Dick stopped painting and looked at Edward.

Edward painted a little more, aware Dick wanted him to say something. He finally stopped and grinned at Dick. "Okay. We'll all go out ... to the lake or movie or somewhere. But you and Carol have got to stop trying to push us together. Sure, I like Betty and she likes me. I said *like*, Dick. Now let's get this finished so we can get someplace cool."

Mrs. Herring and Rachel sat at the kitchen table drinking coffee. The sound of the clock ticking could be heard in the silence.

Mrs. Herring sighed and leaned back in her chair. "Do you feel like eating some breakfast?"

"Not really. I feel like I'm still half asleep." Rachel got up, walked to the cabinet, and refilled her coffee cup. "More coffee?"

"Yes, dear. Thank you. I can't seem to get awake this morning either."

Rachel took the pot to the table and refilled Mrs. Herring's cup. She jumped and spilled coffee on the table when the doorbell rang loudly through the quiet house.

"Oh, I'm sorry. Did any get on you?" Rachel quickly replaced the coffee pot on the counter, and grabbed a dishtowel for the spill.

"No. I'm fine." Mrs. Herring stood up. "Who would be coming to the house this early?" She went to the living room while Rachel wiped up the coffee.

In a moment, Mrs. Herring returned to the kitchen, followed by Mrs. Gaines.

Mrs. Gaines hurried to Rachel's side and embraced her clumsily. Rachel held the wet towel away from both of them.

"Oh, my dear," Mrs. Gaines said as she released Rachel. "I worried about you all night. Didn't get a bit of sleep." She dabbed at her red swollen eyes with a lace handkerchief.

Mrs. Herring pulled another chair out from the table. "Please sit down. Would you like some coffee?"

"Oh, no. I had some when I got up . . . much earlier." Mrs. Gaines sat in the offered chair. "I though for sure you would be up early also. So much to do. But I'm here to help."

Rachel sat back down with her full cup of coffee. "What do you think needs to be done? I know the gifts need to be returned, and I was going to start on that today."

"Yes, of course. All those lovely things . . . meant to be used in Tom's home. And he'll never see them. I do wish he had looked at them the night of the shower."

Rachel sat in the uncomfortable silence that followed. She took a sip of coffee and realized she hadn't put sugar in it. She pulled the sugar bowl to her and stirred one spoon of sugar into the cooling coffee.

She cleared her throat. "I will need your help on the returns. I should have made a list of addresses when we did the thank you cards. Should we mail them all or return them by hand?"

"Most of them we can take to their homes." Mrs. Gaines' spirits seemed to be lifting with the thought of something to do. "People will want to see you, and express their condolences privately. There was such a crowd after the funeral, they couldn't really do that."

Rachel took another drink of her coffee and stood up. "I can get dressed now, and we can start right away if you have time." She took her cup to the sink.

"Yes, that's what I had in mind. I don't have anything planned for today or tomorrow. Hopefully we can get most of them returned then. There are a few relatives out of town that came in for the shower

. . . and would have come back for the wedding." Mrs. Gaines put her handkerchief to her eyes again when fresh tears pooled. She took a deep breath and appeared to get control of herself. "We'll have to mail theirs."

"I'll get dressed, and we can begin right away."

Rachel could hear Mrs. Gaines talking to Mrs. Herring as she went to her room.

I never noticed how loud and grating her voice is. Mrs. Herring's is so soft, it's quite a contrast. I can put up with it a couple more days. I hope we have everything taken care of by this weekend so I can move back to Denton. I'll pick up a paper while we're out today and start looking for an apartment.

Rachel began to think the day would never end. Mrs. Gaines drove her from house to house and the pile of gifts in the back seat slowly dwindled. A few people didn't want their gift returned, but Rachel made sure everything was left at the house it was meant for, even if it had to be put by the door as she hurried out. Some of the people cried and hugged her. Her unhappy face was enough for them. It didn't matter what caused the expression of unhappiness.

Mrs. Gaines took Rachel to a lovely restaurant for lunch, and fussed when Rachel picked at the food and left most of it on her plate.

At last the gifts for that day had all been returned and they started home.

"Would you please stop at that store on the corner." Rachel pointed to the small store ahead of them.

"Of course, dear. Would you prefer going to a larger supermarket?"

"No, this is fine." Rachel hopped from the car as soon as it stopped. She hurried inside, found the paper she wanted, and returned to the car.

Mrs. Gaines looked surprised when she got in. "Don't the Herrings take a newspaper? We take one from Dallas. You're more than welcome to read ours."

"This is a Denton paper," Rachel explained. "I want to start looking for an apartment."

Mrs. Gaines' mouth twisted in a strange frown. "We need to talk about that. Mr. Gaines and I were going to wait until later in the week, after things had calmed down a little. But since it's come up, I'll tell you now." The frown changed to a smile. "You're to move in with us. Tom's room is much too masculine for you, but we'll have a decorator come in and completely redo it. And if you don't feel like going back to college next term, you can stay home. Several of my friends have daughters about your age. They'll help you get into all the activities at the country club and they have their little get-togethers for shopping and bridge. You won't get bored. Do you play bridge? If you don't, I'll teach you."

Rachel stared at Mrs. Gaines. She couldn't believe what she heard.

"Bridge, dear. Do you play?" Mrs. Gaines asked again.

Rachel shook her head to clear it. "No, I don't play bridge." She searched for the right words. "Mrs. Gaines, I appreciate your offer, but I've already made plans to return to Denton. I'll be leaving this weekend."

Mrs. Gaines looked away from the road for a moment to smile at Rachel. "I know you need time to think about this. We'll wait until Saturday to move your things to our home. We've lost a son, but we've gained a daughter. I always wanted a daughter, but after Tom was born I just didn't have time for another child. We'll have such fun together . . . shopping, going to the theatre, all those fun things mothers and daughters do together."

She didn't hear a word I said, Rachel thought.

"You're right. I need time to think about this." Rachel looked straight ahead.

Am I going to let Tom's mother take over my life like Tom did? How can I get out of this? We still have a car load of gifts to return tomorrow or I'd run away tonight. But can I do that? Just run away? She lost her only child. Will my leaving hurt her like losing Tom? I don't want to hurt her. Can anyone help me get out of this?

Mrs. Gaines pulled the car into her own driveway and stopped. "Since this is to be your new home, you may as well stay for dinner."

Rachel hurriedly opened the door and got out. "Thank you, but I need to take a shower and change." Rachel talked as she walked backwards down the drive. "It's been so hot today. I'm really tired."

"All right, dear. I'll see you in the morning." Mrs. Gaines smiled and waved happily.

"Yes, in the morning." Rachel walked fast toward the Herrings. She fought down the urge to run.

When Rachel reached the house and went in, Mrs. Herring was in the kitchen preparing dinner.

"Sit down, Rachel. I'll get you a glass of iced tea. How did today go?"

Rachel lowered herself into a chair at the table and sighed with relief. "I'm glad it's over, and I wish tomorrow was over too."

Mrs. Herring handed Rachel the tall glass of tea with condensation already forming on the sides from the cold contents.

"Thank you. This looks good." Rachel gratefully took the glass.

Mrs. Herring returned to the cabinet and began mixing vegetables for a salad. "You shouldn't wish your life away, wanting things to be over. I know returning all those gifts is an unhappy thing, knowing they were to be in your home with Tom. But all that must be dealt with and put behind you."

Rachel absently wiped the drops of sweat from the side of the glass before taking a drink.

"Mrs. Herring, may I talk to you about something very private? A situation has come up that I don't know how to deal with. I wouldn't want anything I say to get back to Mrs. Gaines, and I don't want you thinking badly of me. There's no one else I can talk to or ask advice from."

Mrs. Herring left the unfinished vegetables on the cabinet, dried her hands on a dishtowel, and came to the table.

"You can talk to me about anything, Rachel. I've only known you these few short weeks, but that's long enough to know you're a good girl. I'll help if I can, and I certainly won't be judgmental. And anything you want kept secret will be."

Rachel hesitated a moment, toying with the glass before looking at Mrs. Herring. "Today, while we were out, Mrs. Gaines told me they expect me to move in with them to live. Not just a visit, but from now on. I don't want to hurt her feelings. She's been hurt so badly by Tom's death, and I certainly don't want to add to that. But I don't want to live with them. I want to go back to Denton and enroll for the fall semester."

"Did you explain that to her?"

"Yes, but she acted like she didn't even hear me. She's just like Tom."

"Were you and Tom having problems before he left for Houston?"

"Mrs. Herring, I'll be honest with you. Tom and I have always had problems, but I was the only one that knew it. He always made all the decisions and plans. It didn't matter what I said or if I wanted something different. He just went ahead like he never heard me . . like I hadn't said a word."

Mrs. Herring looked at Rachel, her eyes full of sadness. "You didn't want to marry Tom, did you?"

Rachel's eyes filled with tears. They rolled down her cheeks unnoticed. "No. Not now. Maybe back in high school I thought I would. That's what my mother wanted. She thought Tom was the perfect man for me. I tried to honor her wishes. Tom reminded me of that when I told him I didn't want to marry him. He made me feel so guilty, I had to say yes. All my life I've tried to do what my parents wanted me to do. I loved them very much, and I miss them so badly it's like a big chunk is missing from the middle of me. It's been a year now, and it still hurts."

Rachel put her head down on her arms on the table and gave in to the tears. Sobs shook her body.

Mrs. Herring moved her chair closer to Rachel and put her arm around her. "Oh, Rachel. I wish you had told me all this sooner. Poor dear. All those problems hanging over you, and you didn't know which way to turn. Well, let me tell you right now, your mother would want you to be happy. I didn't know your mother but I know what kind of daughter she raised, so she must have been a good woman. It's unfortunate Tom died and I know you feel the same way about that, whether you loved him or not. No one would wish that on a young man, or his family. But what matters now is you. You're still alive. You still have a life in front of you. I'll help you work this out with Mrs. Gaines. You know you're welcome to stay here as long as you want to. Go ahead and make plans. After those last gifts are returned you only need to think about what you want and need to do."

Rachel gained control of herself and sat up. She took a paper napkin from the holder in the center of the table and wiped her face.

"Thank you. I really didn't mean to unload all this on you. I'd like to tell you something else, but it's something I haven't told another person and I feel a little afraid to talk about it."

Mrs. Herring patted Rachel's shoulder again. "Anything, dear. It won't go any further than my ears."

Rachel began to talk about Edward, releasing her thoughts and feelings out loud for the first time. As the words tumbled out, her spirits lifted. A feeling of peace and love settled around her.

"And that's why I have to get back to Denton and find him. He doesn't know where I went or what has happened. Somehow I know he's there waiting for me. Waiting for us to be together."

Mrs. Herring took a deep breath, smiled and shook her head.

"My dear, you're a very strong person. You've carried all these feelings by yourself and went about your life just trying to do what you thought was right. Well, you're doing the right thing now. You get back to Denton and find your young man and be happy."

Rachel felt as if a great load had been lifted from her shoulders. "Thank you for listening and understanding." She covered her mouth quickly as a yawn caught her off guard. "This has been a long day. I think I'll take a shower and go to bed."

Mrs. Herring's arm was still around Rachel's shoulders and she gave one more small hug before moving it. "Go take your shower. Dinner should be just about ready when you get out."

"I'm not hungry. Will it hurt your feelings if I just skip tonight?"

Mrs. Herring stood up and smiled. "Of course not. But you have to promise to eat a big breakfast in the morning."

"I promise."

Sleep came quickly for Rachel. Mrs. Herring's words had soothed her battered emotions, but the exhaustion of those emotions remained.

"Sleep soundly, Rachel. Sleep and rest. You have to be strong tomorrow. There is an important lesson you must learn. You must face Mrs. Gaines with courage and tell her what you're going to do. It's wonderful to love people and not want to hurt them. But you also must love yourself and do what you know is right for you. This will not hurt Mrs. Gaines. It may make her unhappy for a while but she will carry on with her life, just as she would if you had never been in it. Every human is responsible for finding their own destiny, their own place in this world. It's time for you to find yours." All through the night Aspen whispered encouragement and hope softly into Rachel's sleeping heart.

Mrs. Gaines arrived at the Herrings early. Rachel and Mrs. Herring were still at the breakfast table lingering over their coffee and talking. Mrs. Gaines was in an obvious good mood.

"I feel so much better this morning," she told Rachel and Mrs. Herring. "I was finally able to sleep last night. Just thinking about having you in the family, Rachel, lifted my spirits. We've always been early risers. We'll have to get you into that habit, too."

Rachel answered Mrs. Gaines but her grin was directed at Mrs. Herring. "I'm not sure that's a habit I really want. I enjoy sleeping in when I have the chance."

"Nonsense. Early rising is a healthy . . ."

Mrs. Herring interrupted. "Would you like some coffee?"

"Oh, no, thank you. I had two cups with breakfast. Rachel and I should get the car loaded and begin. It's going to be terribly hot today. I think there are less things remaining to return than yesterday. Hopefully we can finish earlier."

Rachel stood up from the table, gathered her dirty dishes and carried them to the sink. "May I help with the washing up before I dress?"

"No, no, dear." Mrs. Herring got up and cleared her dishes also. "Go ahead and get ready. I'll take care of these few things." She gave Rachel a significant glance. "You take care of the important things you need to do."

Rachel's hand rested briefly on Mrs. Herring's arm as they stood by the sink. "Thank you. I will." She turned to Mrs. Gaines. "I'll only be a minute."

The gift return did go faster than the day before. At the first two houses they were met by women obviously awakened by their arrival. The next three took the residents from their breakfasts. These five visits were short, made so by the people that answered the door. It seemed to Rachel that Mrs. Gaines' healthy habit of early rising was not shared by her friends and acquaintances.

The gift return continued into the morning. A few people weren't home. By noon the only gifts remaining were those where no one answered their door. For lunch Mrs. Gaines chose a small, elegant tearoom.

The small sandwich on Rachel's plate was delicious, and she ate hungrily. As she put the last bite into her mouth, Rachel glanced up and caught the disapproving frown on Mrs. Gaines' face. Mrs. Gaines's sandwich was only half eaten as she took dainty bites.

Rachel gave a small chuckle. "Sorry. I guess I'm not very lady-like. If something is really good, I kind of make a pig of myself."

Mrs. Gaines smiled condescendingly. "That's all right, my dear. You're a bright young lady, and I'm sure you'll pick up the social graces you need in no time."

Rachel wiped her mouth with her linen napkin and twisted it

absently as she looked down. She took a slow, deep breath, and raised her eyes to look across the small table at Mrs. Gaines.

"Mrs. Gaines, I know how Tom's death has hurt you, and how much you miss him. My heart breaks for you, and I miss him too. But I can't bring him back, and I can't take his place."

Tears began to gather in Mrs. Gaines' eyes. "Oh, my dear. I know you must still be in shock over this. I didn't mean to give the impression that I expected you to replace him. I just know we'll both be happier if we're together to share his memory. In that small way, we can keep him with us always."

Rachel reached across and put her hand on Mrs. Gaines' hand that rested on the table. "I promise you, Tom's memory will always be with me. And I know he'll stay in your heart and mind too, whether I'm around or not." She paused to gather the right words. "I won't be moving in with you and Mr. Gaines. I'm moving back to Denton as soon as I can find an apartment. I'll enroll in the fall semester and try to go on with my life. That doesn't mean I'm going to forget about Tom . . . or his family. Tom would want me to go on with my education and that's what I'm going to do."

For the first time Rachel saw Mrs. Gaines without words. She watched the older woman fight to gain control of her tears. The gray head gave a small nod of understanding without looking up.

Well, it's done, Rachel thought. She wanted to feel relief but an overriding sadness filled her. She swallowed, trying to clear her throat of the lump that hung there.

Mrs. Gaines quietly opened her purse, extracted a bill, laid it on the table, and rose with slow dignity. "I think it's time to return home . . . and you to Mrs. Herring's. I'll call the few we couldn't return the gifts to today, and arrange a time to do that. Don't be concerned. I'm sure I can handle it by myself."

The ride home was in complete silence.

I'm sure I've hurt her feelings terribly, Rachel thought. Will she ever forgive me?

Mrs. Gaines stopped in front of the Herrings'. She turned to Rachel. "You'll always have a place in our hearts, Rachel. Our son loved you so we love you. Don't forget about us. We'd like to hear from you from time to time, and know how you're doing. And if you ever need anything, anything at all, please let us know. We'll help you anyway we can. And if you change your mind, our home is open to you."

Rachel scooted across the seat and put her arms around Mrs. Gaines. "How could I forget you? I'll keep in touch, and send you my address and phone number as soon as I have one. You're to let me know if I can ever help you, too. I'll come back to visit soon . . . you and Mrs. Herring. I've grown to love you both." She kissed the faultlessly made up cheek, gave one more hug, scooted back across the seat, and jumped from the car. She stood on the sidewalk and returned the wave from Mrs. Gaines as she drove away before hurrying into the house.

Mrs. Herring must have been watching from the window because she opened the door as soon as Rachel reached the porch.

"Well, how did it go? I saw what happened in the car. It didn't look like she was mad at you."

"No, she's not mad at me. Hurt maybe, but not mad. She's just a sweet lady that's used to getting her way. I think she understood."

They made their way to the kitchen.

"I guess you've already had lunch," Mrs. Herring said.

Rachel laughed. "Yes, but it was a tiny lady's sandwich and I'm still hungry. Guess I'm not much of a lady."

Mrs. Herring joined in the laughter. "Of course, you're a lady. Well, maybe not. You're probably still just a girl . . . a growing girl. I'll make us both some lunch, and you tell me everything that happened."

Rachel related all that had transpired at lunch while Mrs. Herring prepared their food. While they ate she talked about her plans.

"I'm sure I can find a place. The fall semester is still weeks away. I'll load everything up Friday night and get an early start Saturday. I know Edward will want me to continue my education."

"You will be missed around here." Mrs. Herring's smile was a little melancholy.

"I'll try to get back to visit but, with Edward in my life, I don't know how Mrs. Gaines will react to that. And Edward will be in my life just as soon as I can find him."

Mrs. Herring chuckled. "I have no doubt you will find him. We'll look forward to any visits you can manage. I do want a phone call when you get settled."

"I promise I'll phone."

The two couples sat in a booth mid way of the café. Dick and Carol sat close together on their side. Dick draped his arm around Carol in a comfortable, possessive manner. Edward and Betty got frowns from the waitress as they blew straw wrappers at each other.

"This seems a little crazy," Carol said. "Eating hamburgers this early. Those people over there just ordered eggs and bacon."

Dick gave her an affectionate squeeze. "Nobody said you had to order a hamburger. Eat breakfast if that's what you want. I thought we agreed it was just too hot to bother with food at the lake. We'll swim a little while, come back to town for an early movie, then supper after the movie." Dick hugged Carol tighter, and winked at Edward. "Hey, Ed. What are you and Betty going to do after supper while the two of us go back to the apartment?"

Carol pulled away and swatted Dick on the arm. "Behave yourself. Betty and Edward will be with us all evening."

Edward turned in the booth to face Betty, and grabbed her shoulders, turning her toward him. "Oh, Betty. They aren't ever going to let us be alone."

With a melodramatic gesture, Betty raised the back of her hand to her forehead. "Oh, Edward. However shall we survive this torture?"

Edward pulled her close and kissed her with exaggerated passion. They broke apart laughing. An unusual sound caught Edward's attention. He turned further in the booth to look behind him. Rachel stood only a few feet away. The sound Edward had heard were newspapers being dropped on the floor. They lay scattered at Rachel's feet.

Rachel felt excited and a little sad as she told Mrs. Herring goodbye at the front door. It was early and Mrs. Herring was still in her robe. Mr. Herring had left for work only a few minutes before.

Rachel hugged the woman that had, in the last few weeks, become so dear to her. "Just saying thank you isn't enough for all you've done for me. I can never fully repay you."

"Now don't start talking like that or you'll have us both bawling. Call as soon as you've found a place, and come back the first weekend you have free." Mrs. Herring returned Rachel's hug, turned her around, and gave a gentle push out the door. "The sooner you get started, the sooner you'll have a place to call me about. Take care, my dear, and remember we love you."

"I love you too." Rachel turned and threw a kiss before heading for her car, packed and waiting at the curb.

The short trip to Denton seemed to take forever. Rachel stopped at the first store she came to and bought another newspaper.

I'll stop at that little café up the street for a bite of breakfast and look through the classifieds, she thought.

There was plenty of parking on this early Saturday. She gathered her papers and purse and went in. There was an empty table in the back and she headed for it. Then there he was. Her Edward, only a few feet away .. . kissing a girl. Rachel was unaware she had dropped the papers. She saw him turn and look at her. She backed a few steps, turned and ran.

"Damn keys, where are you?" She fumbled in her purse and found them. As she backed her car out, she saw Edward burst from the front door. "Damn you too." With tears blurring her vision, she sped away.

Edward watched Rachel drive away. His heart felt like it had dropped to the bottom of his boots.

"What am I doing standing here?" He turned and ran back into the café.

"Carol, give me your car keys. I have to catch Rachel."

Betty stood by the side of the booth. "That was Rachel? Come on Carol. We have to help him find her. She saw us kissing, and must think . . . well it's obvious what she must think. Hurry!"

Carol shoved on Dick. "Get up. We can't let her get too far away."

"What about the food?" Dick asked.

"We can eat later." Carol shoved again. "This is more important than food."

Dick got up and motioned to the waitress. "We'll be back. We've got to go solve a love problem first."

The waitress laughed and made a shooing motion with her hands.

Edward was outside first and stood by the driver's door. "Let me drive. I promise I won't wreck or anything."

Carol hesitated, then handed him the car keys. "Any speeding tickets you get are yours."

They all hurriedly climbed into the car. Carol sat in the front with Edward. Edward had the car started and was backing out before the last door was shut. The tires squealed as he started off in the direction Rachel had gone.

Carol leaned forward with her hands on the dash. "Do you have any idea where she might have gone?"

Edward quickly checked the intersection they were coming up on before running the stop sign. "I only know of two people she knows.

Her old landlady and a friend, Toby. I'm not even sure where Toby lives. Never did go have a guitar lesson with him after Rachel dumped me. He lived somewhere close to her old apartment."

Edward quit talking as he squealed the tires around a corner.

He made another turn at the next corner, and was on the street of Rachel's old apartment. Half a block down her car was parked in her old driveway. Edward slowed and pulled in behind it. He wanted her car blocked so she couldn't run away again.

He slammed the car in park and jumped out, leaving the motor running and the door open. He ran up the steps to the porch and jammed his thumb into the doorbell. He didn't let up on the ring until the front door opened.

Mrs. Shaffer stood behind the screen door glaring at Edward. "What do you want?" she asked harshly. "Seems like every time you get around Rachel, you cause trouble and make her cry. Go away and never show your face around here again. I've a good mind to call the police right now."

Edward let his hands drop to his side in a helpless gesture. "Mrs. Shaffer, I don't care if you call the police. I'm going to see Rachel and talk to her. It's not what she thinks. I mean, what she saw. That girl I was with is just a friend. I still love Rachel. I'll always love Rachel. I'll never love anyone else." He put his hands on each side of the door and leaned close to the screen. "Rachel, I love you," he yelled into the house.

Rachel slowly stepped from behind the door and stood by the side of Mrs. Shaffer. She had been standing just out of sight all the time.

"You still love me?" she asked quietly while gazing up at Edward through the screen.

"With all my heart and soul."

Rachel edged past Mrs. Shaffer and pushed the screen open. Edward stepped back to let it open and Rachel was in his arms. They clung tightly to each other. Both were crying, and unaware of their audience or the passage of time.

Edward finally pulled back a little so he could see Rachel's face. He brought one hand to her smiling face and wiped her tears. Rachel did the same to his. Edward heard someone clear their throat. He turned his head and saw that Dick, Carol, and Betty were out of the car and stood at the bottom of the porch steps. He laughed. Carol and Betty had tears streaming down their faces too.

Mrs. Shaffer came out on the porch. She surveyed the gathering with a skeptical frown. "Rachel, don't let this young man talk you into something you don't want."

Rachel turned partially in Edward's arms. "Believe me, Mrs. Shaffer. This is exactly what I want. I've never been happier in my life."

Mrs. Shaffer sighed. "I just don't understand young people anymore." She opened the screen to go in. "If you came to see about the apartment, Rachel, I'm sorry. It's still rented. Now if all of you would find somewhere else to congregate, I can get on with my housework."

Rachel moved from Edward's arms, but kept hold of his hand. "Thank you, Mrs. Shaffer, for everything. We'll get out of your hair now. Bye."

"Let's go," Edward said, and herded the others toward the car, never letting go of Rachel's hand.

He helped Rachel into the back seat and scooted in after her. Betty walked around the car and got in next to Rachel while Carol took over driving again with Dick beside her.

Betty turned slightly in the seat. "Rachel, I'm Betty, and I just want to hug you."

Rachel smiled, a little uncertain, and accepted the hug.

"Edward has talked about you so much, I feel I know you already. He is really crazy about you, but I guess you know that."

Rachel grinned shyly at Edward. "I do now."

Edward pulled her into his arms and kissed her the way he had dreamed about during their long separation. He was oblivious to the others in the car.

Carol waited a few moments before she spoke. "I hate to bother you love birds, but Rachel's car is still here in front of us. Do you plan on just leaving it?"

Edward and Rachel broke apart.

"Oh, my gosh," Rachel said. "I completely forgot about that. Edward, there are boxes in the front seat. Could we move them to this car, or something, so you can ride with me?"

"If that's okay with Carol. We can take them to our apartment. How about it, Carol?"

Carol laughed. "Sure. I figured that's where you two would want to go anyway."

Edward and Dick quickly transferred the boxes, and both cars were finally able to leave Mrs. Shaffer's driveway, and the doubtful Mrs. Shaffer.

"I've so much to tell you," Rachel said as she followed behind Carol's car.

Edward sat close beside Rachel with his arm around her shoulders. "I guess the only thing I have to tell you is how much I love you. And the thing you saw with Betty. Honest, we're just good friends and were horsing around. I told her about you the first time I met her, and she said the two of us might be soul mates. She said that meant two people destined to be together. And we are, so I guess she was right."

Rachel's breath caught in a sob. "And to think we almost weren't." A tear escaped and rolled down her cheek. "Edward, Tom's dead. He was killed in a car wreck just days before the wedding. I'm so mixed up about that. I've known Tom . . . knew Tom since high school. It's just about killed his mother. I hate that it happened, but at the same time I'm so glad I'm free. I didn't love Tom . . . not like I love you."

"Sh-s-s." Edward wiped the tear from her cheek. "No more crying now. We can talk about all that later. Let's just be happy to be together again with nothing to stand between us."

They reached the apartment and carried in the boxes from Carol's car.

"Well, we're still going to get something to eat and go to the lake. Do you two want to come with us?" Dick asked.

Edward looked at Rachel questioningly. She shook her head.

"You all go ahead, and have fun. We're going to stay here and talk," Edward said.

"Talk? Sure." Dick clapped Edward on the back and grinned. "We won't be home 'til late. Promise."

Carol and Betty left first. Dick locked the door with a deliberate motion, and gave Edward a final grin as he closed it behind him.

Edward pulled Rachel into his arms again and kissed her hungrily.

Rachel responded with all the pent up passion she had pushed down for so long. Desire swept through her in a raging torrent but she fought against it and pushed Edward far enough away to speak.

"Edward, we really do have to talk. I have to tell you some things. It's important."

"Rachel, we have all our lives ahead of us to talk. I want you so bad right now, and I've waited so long. I love you. I want to make love to you. I need you worse than I've ever needed anything in my whole life."

Rachel put her fingers to his lips to stop his words. "I know. I feel the same way, but I have to tell you. I'm . . . I'm not a virgin anymore. I was when we met, but Tom . . . well, I'm not now."

A tiny smile curled Edward's mouth. "Neither am I. Rachel, can't you get it through you head? I love you. You. Just like you are. I want to marry you and spend the rest of my life with you. Will you?"

A beautiful smile brought a glow to Rachel's face, and tears shimmered in her eyes. "Yes, I'll marry you, as soon as possible. It can't be soon enough for me."

Edward pulled her close again. "Now that that's settled, no more talking. Make love to me."

He kissed her until their breaths were ragged and their hearts thumped loudly against each other. Trembling, Edward pushed her away far enough to scoop her up in his arms. Their eyes remained locked as he carried her to his bedroom and softly lowered her to the bed.

He lay beside her, pulled her into his arms again and continued the kiss. She moved her hands between them and began to unbutton his shirt. He raised his head and looked down at her. He had never seen such desire on a woman's face and it inflamed him further. His fingers joined hers and the shirt was quickly removed. In unspoken unison they unbuttoned and removed Rachel's shirt and bra.

Unable to stay apart longer, Edward once again lay against her, his bare chest feeling her naked breast against him for the first time. Their lips sought each other, and wave after wave of almost unbearable physical want spread through their bodies. In clumsy haste they parted just long enough to peel off their remaining clothes.

Edward moved to cover Rachel's body with his own and felt her suddenly tense. He looked into her eyes and saw fear.

"Rachel, sweetheart, what's wrong. I won't hurt you. I love you." His words were broken and breathless, strained by the animal lust that possessed him.

Rachel looked into his eyes and the fear left hers, replaced with the look of love and desire that had been there before.

Edward groaned and lowered his lips to hers. He heard her sob when he moved his mouth from her lips to her breast. She arched her back and moved her legs apart, pushing against him with the same urgent desire he felt. He moved his body again, and like two parts of a single entity that had been searching for perfect completion, they joined and became the whole being they were destined to be.

There was no holding back for either of them and they moved

together franticly. Groaning cries raked their throats as the explosion of the all too soon climax joined them. They pressed even closer together, each trying to merge their entire body into the other.

Slowly their hearts regained a normal rhythm. Edward gazed into the eyes of this woman who was part of his soul. He tenderly brushed a tendril of hair from the side of her face and kissed her softly on her cheek.

"I didn't know it was possible to love anyone as much as I love you," he said.

Rachel looked radiant. "I didn't know . . . this kind of love could feel like . . . well, like it does."

Edward slowly turned on his side, bringing Rachel with him to lay close against his body. A comfortable silence settled over them for several minutes before Edward moved his head so he could see Rachel's face.

"I don't mean to sound unromantic," he said, "but I'm hungry. Are you?"

Rachel laughed. "Starving."

With reluctance, they untangled their bodies and moved to sit on the same side of the bed.

Rachel picked her shirt up off the floor and searched the foot of the bed for her underwear. "I think I'll take a shower before I eat, if that's okay."

"Only if I can join you," Edward said, extricating his shorts from his jeans.

Rachel laughed again. "Try to remember we're both hungry while we're in there."

Edward watched her walk across the room to the door. Her slim, shapely, beautiful, and naked body instantly rekindled his desire. "Wow!"

She turned. "Which way is the bathroom?"

Edward jumped up and joined her. "I'll show you. Are you sure you're starving right now?"

Aspen and Willow relaxed on the patio. Their contentment made a soft glow and enhanced the sunbeams that bathed them.

Willow sighed deeply, clasped his hands behind his head and reclined, as if on a lounger. "Guess we can take it easy for a while. I don't know about you, but I could use a vacation. Do you think we'd be missed if we slipped off back home for a visit?"

Aspen gave Willow an indulgent smile. "Better rest while you can." The smile turned pensive. *"There are still hurdles ahead of Rachel and Edward, and that means hurdles for us too."*

Willow sat up straight. "You've got to be kidding. Look at them. They're together. They're happy. What could go wrong now?"

Aspen turned and looked into the kitchen where Rachel and Edward, at last, sat eating. "Something doesn't necessarily have to be wrong to be a hurdle. Humans often interpret happenings in their lives as wrong or a problem when, in truth, it's simply life."

It was late afternoon. Edward and Rachel sat close together on the couch and watched TV. Voices and laughter approached the closed front door. There was the sound of a key in the lock, the knob turned, and the door opened slightly.

Dick called out without looking into the room. "Is it safe?"

Edward grinned at Rachel. "Should I tell him no so they'll go away?"

Rachel laughed. "That wouldn't be very nice. Yes, Dick. It's safe. Of course there's always the chance the building might fall in on you."

Dick swung the door wide and stepped in smiling. "I'll take my chances on that. So how was your day? We had a great time."

Carol and Betty were close behind. Carol hurried to the couch and sat down by Rachel. "Is everything okay now? Did you get all your problems worked out?"

"Everything's fine." Rachel turned to look at Edward. "Should we tell them?"

"Sure. Why not?"

Carol and Betty chimed in together. "Tell us what?"

Rachel smiled smugly, glanced at Edward, then Carol. "We're getting married."

Both girls squealed. Dick rushed forward to shake Edward's hand. There was a moment of confusion with hugs and babbled questions.

Rachel laughed. "Wait a minute. I don't know who to answer first."

Carol grabbed Rachel's hand. "Me first. When?"

"The Friday evening before Labor Day. That way Edward will have three days off for us to spend together."

Betty shoved Carol over on the couch so she could sit too. "Tell us where. You know we all want to be there," she said.

Edward moved his arm from behind Rachel and sat forward on the couch. "I think we'll just run up to Durant, Oklahoma. We can get it all taken care of in one evening."

Dick sat in the chair since there was certainly no more room on the couch. "That's a great idea. After the ceremony, we can get motel rooms, and you two can have a honeymoon night." He winked at Edward. "And the rest of us can just have a fun night."

Carol frowned at Dick. "Forget it, Romeo. Not till there's a ring on this left hand." She shook her hand toward him.

Rachel looked around smiling at all of them. "We want all of you to be there." She leaned forward and looked around Carol at Betty. "Betty, You're the one that said we were soul mates, so I want you to be my maid of honor." She turned to Carol. "And you'll be my bride's maid."

Both girls grinned and nodded.

"What about me?" Dick asked. "Don't I get to carry flowers or something?"

Edward left his seat by Rachel and walked to Dick, extending his hand. "You're my best man, Pal. You know, if you hadn't called me to come down here, I never would've met Rachel. I'll owe you the rest of my life."

Dick stood up and took Edward's hand. They stood for a moment with hands clasped. Edward moved forward and put his left arm around Dick in a hug. Dick returned the hug and they stood for several seconds, patting each other's back.

Edward stepped back, lowered his head and sniffed. He tried to wipe his eyes so no one would realize that tears were accumulating there.

Dick sat back down and quickly rubbed his hand across the bottom of his nose. He cleared his throat. "So, have you two had supper yet?"

Edward grinned at Rachel. "We've kind of been eating off and on all day. But if you all want to go out to eat, we'll go with you and get a bite." He sat back down by Rachel.

Rachel jumped up. "Let me freshen up a bit and comb my hair."

Carol and Betty stood up. "Yeah, us too," Carol said.

The three girls headed for the bathroom. Dick and Edward grinned at each other when they heard the whispers and giggles start as soon as the girls were in the hall.

When the bathroom door was shut, and the living room was still and quiet, Dick said, "Congratulations, Edward. I don't doubt for a minute that Rachel's the right girl for you. I know the two of you are going to grow old together," he paused, "and probably have twenty kids before you get old."

Edward leaned his head back against the couch and looked at the ceiling. "Yeah, I'm going to stay with that girl till I die." He grinned, "But maybe only ten or twelve kids."

Edward and Rachel lifted the last boxes from her car and carried them into the apartment. They stacked them in Edward's room along with the others they had brought in.

Rachel looked at the boxes and chewed on her lower lip. "Do you think Dick thinks badly of me because I'm moving in here with you before we're married?"

"No, of course not," Edward said. "It would be dumb for you to try to get an apartment for a couple of weeks. And if you keep cooking for us like you did for breakfast this morning, he'll be begging you to marry him." He paused. "Seriously, I talked to him about this last night. He really likes you and wants us to keep living here after we're married if you have no problem with that."

A small smile curled Rachel's lips. "I don't care where I live as long as it's with you." She opened one of the boxes marked 'clothes', and began to look through the contents. "I can help with the rent and bills. Mother and Daddy left me enough to pay for everything and finish college."

"Whoa! You mean I got me a rich woman, and didn't even know it?" Edward laughed, and moved behind Rachel, encircling her waist with his arms.

Rachel twisted around and faced him. She put her arms around his neck. "No, silly. Not rich, but enough to get a degree so I can get a good job somewhere."

Her expression turned serious. "What about your family? What will they say about us living together now?"

Edward's expression changed to match Rachel's. "You have a point there." He moved away from Rachel and sat on the edge of the bed. "Mom wouldn't understand at all. I think Pete and Dad would but Mom would have the last say." He looked up at Rachel. "So to protect your good name, we won't tell them. Ohio is a long way off, and they just don't need to know."

Rachel went to sit beside Edward. "Are you going to call and tell them we're getting married? Do you think they'll come down for the wedding?"

"I doubt it. Well, Pete might. You'll like him, Rachel. He's a good big brother. In fact, I'm sure you'll like all my family. Next vacation time I get, that's where we'll go. I want to show you off to them."

Rachel chuckled and stood up. "Okay. We'll live in sin secretly for the next couple of weeks. That kind of gets me excited."

Edward grabbed her and pulled her back down on the bed. "How excited?"

The next afternoon Rachel called Mrs. Herring and told her about finding Edward and the wedding plans. She gave the address and phone number of where she was. Mrs. Herring happily took all the information and secretly surmised Edward probably had the same address.

Dick and Edward came in laughing. Dick headed for his room. "Hi, Rachel. I'm going to grab some clean clothes and take a quick shower. Man, was it hot today. I'm soaking wet with sweat. I'll hurry, Edward. By the time you get through saying hi to your darlin', I'll be through."

Grinning, Edward waved Dick away and went to sit by Rachel on the couch. "How was your day, Sweetheart? I'm not going to hug you right now. I'm too sweaty and dirty."

Rachel sat with her feet propped up on the coffee table and didn't raise her face to his greeting.

Alarmed, Edward took her chin in his hand and turned her face toward him. "What's wrong, Honey?"

Rachel pulled her face from his hand and looked down at her hands clasped in her lap without replying.

Edward turned on the couch to face her. "For God's sake, Rachel. Tell me what's wrong."

Rachel took a deep breath and let it out with a sigh. "You know I was going to the doctor today to get a check up and see about some kind of birth control." She didn't continue.

"Is something wrong with you? Are you sick? Rachel, we're getting married in two days. You have to tell me." Edward's voice was on the edge of panic now.

Rachel continued to look down. Tears were streaming from her eyes. "It's too late."

"Too late? What are you talking about?" Edward grabbed her shoulders and turned her to face him.

"It's too late for birth control. I'm pregnant."

Edward blinked several times in stunned silence. A big grin spread across his face, and he pulled her into his arms.

"Sh-h, Honey. That's not anything to cry about. We're just starting a family a little earlier than we planned. It'll be great." He moved her away so he could wipe the tears from her face. "I'm tickled pink."

Rachel looked into his eyes with desperation. "You don't understand. It's Tom's"

Edward slowly lowered his arms from around Rachel and sat up straight. "Tom's?"

Rachel again lowered her eyes. "Remember, I told you I wasn't a virgin. I didn't have sex with him because I wanted to. He made me. The son-of-a-bitch got me pregnant." She covered her face with her hands and sobbed.

Edward felt frozen. He wanted to move, to stand up, but his legs wouldn't obey. He suddenly hit his legs with both fists and stood up. He backed toward the door. Rachel looked up at him, her face contorted with agony.

"I've . . . I've got to think . . . about this," Edward said and turned. With quick strides, he went out the door. He didn't notice where he walked. His mind spun with questions. The questions overlapped before he could begin to understand or think about the answer to even one.

Fatigue finally hit him, and he sagged against the building he stood in front of. As if waking from sleep, he looked around and saw it was almost night. Streetlights had come on. He saw the building he leaned against was a store. He pushed away from the wall that supported him, went in, and bought a pack of cigarettes and a small box of matches. When he came out he realized he was next door to the café where he had first seen Rachel back in Denton. A few steps brought him to the door of the café, and he went in. There were few customers and many vacant tables and booths. He made his way to a booth in the back and sat down.

The waitress was immediately by his side. "What can I get you, son?"

He looked up at the friendly face, bordered by graying hair. "Just coffee, please."

The coffee was quickly put before him, and the waitress left to refill another customer's cup.

Edward took the pack of cigarettes out of his pocket and lit one. Okay, he thought as he sipped the hot coffee. Rachel's pregnant ... and it's not mine. But I still love her. What did she say? He made her? He raped her. He was a son-of-a-bitch. It's a good thing he's dead or I'd have to go kill 'im. How will I feel about his kid?

"Ready for a refill?"

Edward blinked and looked up. He hadn't seen the waitress walk up beside him. "Yes, thank you."

She refilled his cup and stood there a moment, as if she wanted to say something. Edward looked at her questioningly.

She gave him a wry smile. "You got problems, son?"

He looked up at her a few seconds before answering. "Yes, ma'am. Guess I do."

She nodded once, and went to the cash register at the front of the cafe to take money from the last customer. Edward had not noticed when the others left. She followed that customer to the front door, locked it behind him, and flipped the open sign to closed.

Edward stood up, and dug in his pocket for money. "I'm sorry. I didn't know it was time to close. I'll get out of your hair."

"Just sit back down, son. I'm going to join you for a cup of coffee. It's been a long day. I'm ready to get off my feet for a while, and have a little conversation." She talked as she came toward the booth, and stopped briefly to pick up a coffee cup from the stack behind the counter and the half full coffee pot.

Edward was a little confused. He didn't know this motherly looking woman, and he didn't particularly want to talk to her.

She scooted into the other side of the booth, and poured her cup full. She refilled Edward's cup that was half empty and set the pot on the table.

"Where're you from, son?"

"Ohio."

"You're a long way from home. I see by your uniform you work here at the college. Been here long?"

"No ma'am. Just a few months." Edward couldn't think of anyway he could get up and leave.

"You got a girlfriend?"

"Well, I . . I guess," Edward stammered. He didn't like the question, and began to feel resentful.

That's none of your business, old woman, he thought.

"Now, don't get your fur all ruffled up. If you were back home in Ohio, would you talk to your mother about your problems? And I'd venture to guess it's about your girlfriend."

Edward felt tears start to gather in his eyes, and slumped down in his seat.

"My name is Belle," the waitress said, and reached across to pat Edward's hand that lay on the table next to his cup. "Why don't you just pretend you're talking to your mother, and tell me what's got you so tore up."

The words seemed to pour out of Edward of their on accord. The story of Rachel unfolded . . . their meeting, and the love they had felt for each other from the very first . . . Tom, and the engagement he couldn't understand . . . Tom's death, and Rachel's return . . . the wedding plans . . . the unexpected news of Rachel's pregnancy, conceived in rape.

"And I believe her about that," Edward said emphatically. "Rachel wouldn't lie to me."

Belle waited quietly for a moment to see if he had more to add. "You know, she could of just married you and not told you about being pregnant till later."

Edward's head jerked up, and he looked across at Belle, but remained silent. He hadn't thought about that.

"You say you love this girl," Belle continued. "Looks to me like you'd love any baby she had just as much. It's part of her, you know."

A slow smile spread across Edward's lips and spread to his eyes. He lifted his coffee cup in a toast. "Belle, you're absolutely right."

Belle laughed and lifted hers. The heavy pottery cups met with a clunk. They each took a drink of their coffee and put the cups on the table.

"Now then, son," Belle said. "I think it's time you got back to that sweet girl and tell her you love her and the baby."

Edward scooted out of the booth and stood up. "Yes, ma'am. You're right again. Thanks." He stopped at the door and turned, digging in his pocket. "I almost forgot to pay for the coffee."

Belle waved it away. "Forget it, and get out of here. It's on the house."

Edward unlocked the door and hurried out smiling broadly, turned toward the apartment, and ran.

Willow shook her hand. "Thanks, Belle. You sure handled that problem for me."

"I didn't do it for you. Sibyl has been after me to get involved ever since this started. She's caused a lot of disturbance and They told me to do something. Then Tom got there and really started having fits when he realized what he had done. It has not been the peaceful place it should be."

"Well, thanks anyway. Edward's happy. Rachel will be happy, once he gets home to her, and that makes me happy and my job easier."

"You're welcome. Now you better get after him to make sure he doesn't run out in front of a car in his haste."

Willow waved and hurried after Edward.

Rachel didn't hear Dick come out of the bathroom and was not aware of his presence until he spoke.

"My God! What's happened? Where's Edward?"

Rachel's sobs increased. She jumped from the couch, rushed by him into the bedroom, and slammed the door without answering. She threw herself on the bed and gave in completely to the anguish she felt.

"I'm so sorry Edward," she said aloud. "I never should have agreed to marry Tom. I never should have let him touch me. Are you happy now, Mother? I tried to do what you wanted, and look where it's got me." She pressed her face into the pillow and groaned. "I love you Edward. I'll always love you."

Rachel's sobs slowed, and the tears finally stopped. She turned over and reached for a tissue on the nightstand, blew her nose and wiped her eyes.

"All right, girl. Get a hold on yourself. You've got to figure out what you're going to do."

Rachel stared at the ceiling for a long while thinking.

I could go back and live with the Gaines'. I'm sure it would thrill Mrs. Gaines to know Tom was going to have a child. This child will be their only heir. I wouldn't have to worry about how to take care of it, or its college money, or anything. But they'd take it away from me. Maybe not physically, but they would spoil it so rotten, it would do whatever they said, just to keep the goodies coming. It would grow up just like Tom.

At that thought, Rachel sat up, and swung her legs off the side of the bed. "Oh no. That's not going to happen to you, kid." She put her hands on her stomach. "I'll take care of you by myself, and you'll grow up good, and independent, and nice, and care about other people. In the morning I'll find a place for us to live, and we'll be fine. Don't worry, baby. Everything's going to be okay."

She got up and began to pull her clothes out of the dresser drawers and pile them on the bed. "I wish I hadn't thrown away the boxes when I unpacked. I'll just have to find some more tomorrow."

Her industrious activity was interrupted by a knock on the door.

"Rachel, It's Dick. Can I come in?"

Rachel sighed. "Sure Dick, come on in." Her voice was resigned and unhappy.

Dick opened the door slowly and stepped into the room. "Would you mind telling me what happened. After all the trouble you and Edward had trying to get together, now it looks like your leaving. You're going to be married in two days. What could be so bad that you have to leave now? Do you still love Edward? I know he still loves you."

"Of course I still love Edward." Rachel yanked clothes out of the closet. "Something has happened, and Edward doesn't love me anymore. He left, didn't he?"

Dick stepped in front of Rachel and grabbed her by the shoulders as she walked to the bed with her arms full of clothes. "Stop that right now. There isn't anything bad enough to make Edward stop loving you. Did he say that? Did he say he didn't love you?" He gave her a little shake.

Rachel looked down, unable to meet his gaze. "No, he didn't say that. But he left. He just walked out."

"Well, I know Edward about as good as a person can know another person. I'm telling you right now he loves you. He may have had to work something out in his head. That's the only reason I can think of for him to do that. Did he say anything?"

"That's what he said, he had to think about it." Rachel leaned her head over the clothes in her arms, and put her forehead on Dick's chest. "Dick, what am I going to do?"

"I'll tell you exactly what you're going to do. You're going to stop this nonsense with the clothes. I'll help you put them back. Then we'll go in the living room and wait for Edward to get back. You'll see. He'll have his head on straight, and he'll tell you himself that he still loves you, and wants to marry you." He gave her another little shake and pushed her back.

Rachel looked up with a teary smile. "You really believe that, don't you Dick?"

"I don't just believe it. I know it."

"Thanks. You're a good friend . . . to both of us."

Edward shoved open the door and staggered in his haste to get into the apartment. Rachel sat on the couch and Dick was in the chair. He breathed heavily with his mouth open. He had run all the way from the café, and was wet with sweat. Rachel looked up at him expectantly. Fear and doubt shadowed her face. He walked to the couch and fell to his knees before her.

"I'm sorry. I'm so sorry." He laid his head over on her legs. "I love you. Nothing else is important. I'll always love you, and any children you bring into this world." He raised his head and looked up at her, tears streaming down his cheeks. "Forgive me for running off like that. Please say you'll still marry me Friday?"

Rachel put her hands on his cheeks, her tears matching his. "Of course I'll marry you. I love you." A huge smile washed over her face. All the fear and doubt vanished. "In fact, you'd have a hard time getting rid of me. Sweetie, You're stuck with me for the rest of you life."

Even from his awkward position on the floor, Edward was able to wrap his arms around Rachel and pull her close.

Dick cleared his throat. "I hate to disturb you two lovebirds, but my stomach just reminded me that none of us have had supper. You may can live on love right now, but I need some real food."

Edward and Rachel parted laughing. They wiped the tears from each other's faces.

He stood up and pulled Rachel up with him. "I've got to take a shower and put some clean clothes on. What do we have in the kitchen that will be fast and easy?"

Dick headed for the kitchen. "Sandwiches."

Rachel gave Edward a tiny kiss on the lips. "Go get clean. I'll have a sandwich ready for you when you get out."

Edward left the room and Rachel joined Dick in the kitchen. Dick pulled food from the refrigerator and put it on the table. Rachel got the bread from the cabinet. Neither said anything until they were at the table.

Rachel put the knife down she had used to smear mustard on bread. "Dick, I guess you've probably figured out most of what this is all about."

Dick studied her seriously as he chewed. He swallowed. "I'd venture a guess that you're pregnant and it's not Edward's."

Rachel looked down, no longer able to meet his gaze. "Do you think I'm a tramp now?"

Dick almost choked on the bite he had in his mouth. "My God, no." He laid his sandwich down and stared hard at Rachel until she finally looked up at him. "I heard enough about that Tom character to pretty much fill in most of the details, and I don't need you to tell me anything more. You and Edward are going to get married Friday night, and Uncle Dick is going to be there for all the babies you two have. That includes this first one that's coming along pretty soon." He picked up his sandwich and put it back down. "Rachel, you belong to Edward, so in a way you belong to me too. Edward and I have been best friends almost all our lives. Like it or not, I'm part of the package."

Rachel got up, stepped behind Dick, and put her arms around him. "I'm glad you're part of the package. I love you Dick. I feel like I'm getting a husband and a big brother."

Edward walked into the kitchen and grinned. "Glad to see my two favorite people getting along."

Rachel turned and went into his arms. "Thank you for sharing your best friend with me."

"Anytime," Edward said. "Got a sandwich ready for me?"

"No. I've been too busy hugging Dick. Sit down. It won't take a minute."

Thursday evening Edward sat back in his chair and put his crumpled paper napkin beside his plate. "That was a great supper, Rachel. I'm getting a beautiful woman and a good cook. How lucky can I get? Now I want to take us all out for desert."

"Thanks. You want desert after that meal you just ate?" Rachel asked.

"Mainly I want you to meet someone . . . the waitress at the café. She's a sweet old gal. Her name's Belle, and she's the one that sent me running back home last night." Edward got up and took his plate to the sink.

Dick followed him with his own plate. "I could use a piece of that pie they have there."

Rachel got up and stacked her plate with theirs. "Okay, but I don't think I could hold desert. I'll just have a coke."

They piled into Dick's pickup and drove to the café. The evening rush was over. They parked close to the front and went in. The café was almost empty. They chose a booth in the front. A young, dark haired waitress brought menus and water as soon as they were seated. Her nametag said 'June'.

Edward declined the menu. "I just want some chocolate pie and coffee. Is Belle working tonight?"

June looked puzzled. "Nobody named Belle works here."

"Sure she does. She waited on me last night, and closed up."

"You must have been at another café. We close at two on Wednesdays. I was here when we closed so I know you weren't here." June turned to Dick. "Would you like pie and coffee too?"

"Yeah, but I want pecan."

"And you ma'am?"

"I'll just have a coke."

June left to fill the order.

Edward stared down at the table and rubbed his forehead. "I know this is the right place. I was sitting right back there." He got up from the table. "Just a minute. I want to check something." He went out the front door, walked a few feet, and checked the building next to the cafe. Perplexed, he came back in and sat down. "The store is next door where I bought cigarettes. I came out of it and right in here."

June brought the pie and drinks.

Dick smiled at her. "Thanks, honey." He picked up his fork and motioned toward the door with it. "The sign there on the door says they're closed Wednesday at two. You were pretty rattled last night so don't worry about it." He took a bite of pie.

Rachel put her arm around Edward's shoulders and hugged gently. "Dick's right. Somewhere in this town is a café that's open on Wednesday nights with a store beside it. And the waitress at that café is named Belle. Eat your pie." She laughed. "You're probably eating your last desert as a single man, so you better enjoy it."

Edward smiled at Rachel and began to eat.

I know this is the right place, he thought. Something funny is going on, or I'm losing my mind. Belle, wherever you are now, thanks for being here for me last night.

Aspen smiled at Rachel. He could feel her happiness. "Thanks, Belle," Aspen said to the glow that hovered beside him.

"No thanks needed. I explained all this to Willow last night. Sibyl was running around like crazy trying to find someway to help her daughter, and bugging me constantly to do something. She really loves that girl." Belle laughed. "Everyone there was telling me to do something. When Tom arrived, and both of them felt responsible for all the problems and heartache Rachel had encountered, you wouldn't believe the turmoil the two of them caused."

Aspen laughed too. "They were both strong willed humans. It sounds like they still are."

Willow smiled. He was having trouble keeping his glow under control. Edward's happiness was almost too much to contain.

"Can we relax a while now, or is there more hard work coming up?"

"Yes, you can relax for a while. There will be problems to come in the years ahead, but maybe not as big as the ones they've had getting started together. As long as humans have free will, they will have problems." Aspen couldn't resist touching Rachel's head lightly. He let the love she felt flow through him. That feeling was the reason he wanted to keep being a guardian.

Friday morning Rachel stood by the table with curlers in her hair. Several towels were spread on the table, and she used it as an ironing board. The dress she had bought the day before needed a little touch to take out a few wrinkles. The dress shirt she had gotten for Edward was already pressed and hung on a hanger over the doorsill. She glanced at the clock.

Eleven o'clock, she thought. I hope Edward and Dick can take off at two like they wanted to. Her thoughts were interrupted by the ringing phone.

"Hello."

"Rachel?"

"Yes, who is this?"

"Pete. Edward's brother."

"Oh, Pete. Hi. Edward won't be home for another three hours. Can he call you then?"

"No, he can say hello in person. I'm in Denton. You two didn't think you were going to do this without me, did you? I just need directions to your apartment."

Rachel almost squealed her reply. "That's wonderful! Edward is just going to bust."

She got his location and gave him the directions. He wasn't far away. Ten minutes later she threw the door open at his knock, and stood grinning at him.

Pete laughed, grabbed her around the waist, lifted her off the floor and swung her around. "You're just as pretty as Edward said you were." He put her down.

"Well, you're pretty too, and Edward never told me that. Why didn't you let us know you were coming?"

"I just woke up early yesterday morning and decided I was coming. I called my boss, went by and had breakfast with Mom and Dad, and headed out."

"I'm very glad you did. Edward is going to be so excited."

Rachel made a pot of coffee, and they continued to talk as she finished pressing her dress. The three hours that Rachel had thought would drag flew by. A few minutes after two o'clock, Edward and Dick could be heard laughing and talking as they approached the door.

Edward opened the door and froze with his mouth hanging open. "Pete, you-son-of-a-gun," he yelled, and bounded across the room to grab his brother in a bear hug. "I just told Dick that car in the parking lot is like my brother's."

Dick followed close behind and pumped Pete's hand when Edward finally released him. With all the babbling commotion, no one noticed when Carol and Betty came through the still open door. After a few minutes, things calmed down slightly, and Carol and Betty were introduced to Pete.

"All of this is wonderful," Rachel said, "but we need to get ready."

"I'll take the shower first," Dick said. "It doesn't take me long. That'll give you a few more minutes with Pete."

An hour later they all left the apartment and gathered on the sidewalk.

Edward had his arm around Rachel's waist. "We're going in Rachel's car cause we won't be coming back here tonight." He gave her a squeeze.

"We're going on our honeymoon." He suddenly frowned and looked at Pete. "Do you mind coming back here tonight with Dick? We'll come on back tomorrow some time. How long can you stay?"

"I'm going to stay 'til Monday. I took all next week off for vacation. I think I'll leave here Monday and drive over to Kentucky to visit some of our cousins. None of us have been to see them in three or four years."

Edward grinned. "That's great. Okay now, who's going to ride with who to Oklahoma?"

Carol and Dick got in the front seat of her car that was parked next to Rachel's, and Pete and Betty got in the back. Edward heard them laughing as he opened the passenger door of Rachel's car and bowed deeply.

"You're carriage awaits, my lady," he said.

"Thank you, kind sir." Rachel got in.

Amid merriment and laughter, the two cars headed for Durant, Oklahoma.

The drive to Durant didn't take long. The sunny afternoon made the time fly by. Edward stopped at the first small building he saw displaying a 'Marriage Information' sign. The middle-aged man inside took over.

He was dressed for the last of the summer heat in a short sleeve shirt and slacks. He was casual and friendly as he led the two Texas cars around town for blood tests, and to get the license. His final stop was in front of an old rock church. The church was built on the side of a hill, and a long rock staircase led up to double doors. When the man got out of his car, he opened his back door and reached into the back seat. First he brought out a tie and put it on. A coat followed that. The final thing he brought out was a Bible.

"Oh, my gosh," Edward said. "He's the preacher. I didn't say any bad words around him, did I?"

Rachel laughed. "No, you were a perfect gentleman," she assured him.

The six followed the coated man up the steps, through the double doors, and to the front of the beautiful, old church.

Edward held Rachel's right hand tightly, and they stopped when the minister stopped and turned to face them. Dick took his place to Edward's right, and Pete stepped up beside Dick. Betty moved to stand beside Rachel and Carol stood next to Betty.

The late afternoon sunrays poured through the stained glass

171

windows high in the front wall of the church sending rainbow light over the people below. Edward and Rachel looked at each other.

"Beautiful light," Rachel whispered.

"Beautiful you in the light," Edward responded, also in a whisper. He was afraid if he spoke too loud, the magic light would disappear.

The minister opened his Bible. "Dearly Beloved,"

Aspen floated in the rainbow rays with Willow beside him. The other four guardians were there also, lending their own glow to Aspen's and Willow's. This was the time they had all worked and waited for. There was another increase in the beautiful glowing light. Aspen turned to see another guardian had joined them.

He moved slightly to take the newcomer's hand. "I'm glad you could make it, Belle."

"Wouldn't have missed it for the world." Belle took her place with the others.

Rachel moved drowsily in Edward's arms, cuddling closer. The motel bed was comfortable, and they had made love on it until their bodies insisted they get a little sleep.

"Edward?" she murmured.

"H-m-m?"

"Did I hear Pete say you had cousins in Kentucky?"

"Yeah," he yawned and turned slightly, putting his other arm over Rachel. He didn't open his eyes.

"Can we go there someday?"

"Sure."

The answer was little more than a sigh. Rachel smiled as she heard Edward's breathing become almost a snore. She closed her eyes and fell asleep thinking about the pictures she had seen in the book. She could see Edward by her side as they walked through the beautiful woodlands of the Kentucky mountains.

Just The Beginning

Epilog

Mrs. Gaines sat at the Herrings breakfast table and stirred the tea in her cup with an agitated vigor. Bea Herring finally touched her hand softly to stop the motion.

"Bea, I just can't accept this. Rachel has obviously suffered a complete mental breakdown from Tom's death. There must be something we can do legally to put a stop to this Edward thing and get Rachel in some kind of hospital until she gets her senses back. Married! No, I can't accept this. We've got to help the girl get out of it." She began stirring the tea again.

Bea Herring looked down at her cup and tried to hide the smile she knew Mrs. Gaines wouldn't understand. Rachel and Edward had come for a brief visit the week after their wedding.

"He seems like a very nice young man and Rachel appeared to be happy. Maybe we shouldn't be so hasty in our judgment."

Mrs. Gaines began to stir her tea again. "Rachel was so vague about where or when she met him. I know she said he works at the college but doing what? Does he teach or clean the toilets?"

Bea patted Mrs. Gaines hand again to stop the stirring. "She promised to keep in touch and I really think she will. We'll both be there to help her if she ever needs us."

"If the poor dear will ask for help. She's so independent and hard headed. Thank God I never had that problem with Tom. He was always ready to do what ever I asked him to do."

Bea got up and took her cup to the sink. She was ready for this visit

173

to be over. "Yes, Tom was an exceptional young man. You were fortunate to have had him for a son."

Mrs. Gaines relinquished her tea cup and prepared to leave. "You will let me know if you hear anything from Rachel and I'll do the same."

"Of course I will. Now go on home and try to get some rest."

Bea watched from her front door as Mrs. Gaines started her walk home.

"Lord, be with this well meaning woman and try to give her some happiness or at least peace."

Almost a year after the wedding Edward and Rachel did visit Kentucky on their way home from a vacation in Ohio. After that visit, they returned to Denton just long enough to pack their belongings in preparation to move to Kentucky. They stayed in Denton long enough to witness Dick and Carol's wedding. A year after that Dick and Carol moved into a small house a short way up the hollow from Edward and Rachel. A few years after that, they were joined by Pete and his wife, Betty, whom he had courted by mail and phone calls after he went back to Ohio.

If you should be driving through Kentucky sometime, outside a nice sized town with a lovely small college, enjoying the morning mist that looks smoky at the base of the mountains, and turn up a little road in a certain hollow, keep your eyes open for a log cabin. It has been added onto several times, and now sprawls on the side of the hill, just off the road. A big porch runs all the way across the front, and you're likely to see an old couple sitting there. He may be playing a guitar, and she'll probably have a book in her hands. A sign on a post by the road will tell you hand made furniture and crafts are sold here.

If your drive is on a Saturday or Sunday, there will be cars parked in the drive, sometimes as many as six. The six children, and their spouses and the grandchildren visit often. They've scattered out, some even to other states, but they always like to come home to see Mom and Dad.

But if your drive is on a weekday, drive slowly and look closely at the couple on the porch. Even in the still air down in the hollow, a breeze will move the gray hair on both their heads. It's as if some unseen fan is giving them a breeze, or perhaps it's just angel wings.